POINT
SF

STRANGE INVADERS

Stan Nicholls

■SCHOLASTIC

For Owen Brown and Ben Brown, with love.
Because I always smile when I think of you.

Scholastic Children's Books,
7–9 Pratt Street, London NW1 0AE, UK
a division of Scholastic Publications Ltd
London ~ New York ~ Toronto ~ Sydney ~ Auckland

Published by Scholastic Publications Ltd, 1995

Copyright © Stan Nicholls, 1995

ISBN 0 590 13102 8

Typeset by DP Photosetting, Aylesbury, Bucks
Printed by Cox & Wyman Ltd, Reading, Berks

10 9 8 7 6 5 4 3 2 1

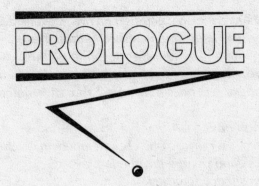

PROLOGUE

It could have been the darkest place on Earth.

No moon lit the velvety night and all below was a shapeless patchwork of greys. Strands of thick mist drifted sluggishly across the desolate landscape. Only the spire of a distant church pierced the gloom, a ghostly pale needle against ebony blackness.

A glint of dim light winked for a fraction of a second in the heart of a barren cloud.

The leaves of gaunt trees rustled softly in a puff of wind as a timorous rabbit darted for the shelter of its burrow. Far away, the haunting cry of a nocturnal bird rose and fell before deathly quiet renewed its slumbering embrace.

A red streak cut across the sky.

It was followed by another. And another. Dozens

of brilliant crimson gashes sliced the heavens, faded to pinkish orange, and vanished from sight.

Something like a whisper began to fill the air.

It grew to a high-pitched whistle, and became a shrieking howl until a dull impact abruptly smothered it.

Tranquillity was ripped apart as the noises were repeated. A rain of objects screamed through the darkness and pummelled the land.

Then silence returned.

But not for long. The sound of an approaching vehicle broke the new calm.

Churning the fog, gears grinding, a covered jeep with dipped headlights bounced out of the shadows. It rolled to a halt and the engine died. The canvas flap at the rear was pulled aside and two men emerged. A third slid out of the driver's seat.

They were dressed in black.

The driver reached back into the cab and brought out two flashlights and two empty sacks. He handed one of each to the others, turned again to get a torch and sack for himself, and slammed the door.

They stood motionless, gazing intently into the surrounding murk. Not one word was spoken. A witness to the scene would have been struck by the men's complete immobility, and their unnaturally straight, rigid postures.

If they didn't know better, anyone watching might even think the men weren't breathing.

Finally, as though by unspoken agreement, the trio stirred. Still mute, they pointed their torches at the ground and slowly fanned out in different directions. Every few yards one of them stooped to look at something. After examining each find they either moved on or picked it up and dropped it into the sack.

Half an hour later, seemingly obeying an instruction no one else could hear, they returned to their starting point at exactly the same time.

As the two passengers settled themselves in the back of the truck, gently cradling the bulging sacks, the driver paused and looked up at the dismal sky. His blank face gave no hint of what he was thinking. But as he eased into the front seat and reached for the ignition key, he allowed himself a fleeting, utterly cold smile.

The jeep pulled away, leaving Gallows Moor to brood in peace.

The last fiery streaks dissolved in the sky beyond the spire of Leyswood parish church.

Owen stretched and moved from the window. The show was over for another night. For more than a week he had watched the strange aerial displays above the moor, and was still no wiser about what they were. At least he wasn't alone in that. *Nobody* seemed to know what was going on. He pushed the mystery from his mind. There were more important things to concern him.

Lugging the chair to his desk, he turned on the synthesizer. The VDU over it flickered and displayed a ruled page with musical symbols dotting the first two lines. He studied the screen for a while before clicking-in the drum machine program. A low-volume bass rhythm thumped from the speakers on either side of the room and he idly tapped the edge of the keyboard with one finger. The piece wasn't too bad, but it needed a lot more work, and he especially wanted to get this particular track on the demo. Owen creased his brow as he concentrated on counting beats to the bar.

He didn't hear his father come in.

One moment he was alone, the next, Stewart Carter was standing stiffly beside him. He didn't speak, and his thick-lensed spectacles framed completely vacant, watery eyes. With a thud, he deposited a green mug at Owen's elbow, avoiding his son's gaze. Then he turned and shuffled away. Owen, taken aback at first, now found his tongue.

"Er . . . thanks, Dad."

His father didn't answer or look back. The door slammed behind him. Owen frowned. Why was he behaving so . . . *coldly*? What had brought about such a change in his normally outgoing personality? Perhaps it had something to do with Owen's mother being in Canada. Maybe his dad couldn't cope. True, he never was much good at household chores, but that didn't explain his grumpy attitude. Could he be ill?

Lifting the mug, Owen took a sip. And gagged. He scrutinized the contents. Coffee granules floated in a crunchy brown scum. His father had made the drink with cold water. Revolted, he slammed it down again. What was *wrong* with him?

The doorbell rang. He was about to go downstairs when he heard a familiar voice in the hallway. Someone clambered noisily up the staircase. His bedroom door flew open and his girlfriend, Leigh, swept in. Breathless as usual, she threw aside her shoulder bag and shrugged off her knee-length, black velvet jacket. She shook out her long auburn hair.

"Hi, Owen!" She kissed him on the cheek. He grinned and hit a button on the synthesizer. The music expired. Sweeping a pile of computer magazines from the only other chair, she fell into it and plonked her lace-booted feet on the edge of his desk. Owen always smiled when he saw those enormous boots, and once made the mistake of telling Leigh she looked like Godzilla when she wore them. She hadn't seen the joke.

"Your dad's a bit moody, isn't he?"

His expression soured. "Tell me about it. What did he say?"

"Nothing. That's the point. Just stood there like a dummy and stared at me. Have I done something to upset him?"

"No. But maybe *I* have. He's acting pretty weird at the moment."

"I noticed that."

"What do you mean?"

She gave him one of her lopsided grins.

"You never see further than your music gizmos, do you, Owen? I had to bite my tongue when he let me in."

"Why?"

Leigh giggled. "Because your gonzo dad's wearing his shoes on the wrong feet, that's why."

The look on his face wiped the grin off her's. "What's wrong?" she asked.

"I'm not sure. *You* know my father, Leigh. Really easy-going, never loses his temper; a good laugh usually. But he's been ... well, *odd*, lately. Now you're telling me he can't even dress himself properly."

"I expect it's just your mum going off to your cousin's wedding. Your dad's not exactly a New Man when it comes to running a home, is he?"

"That's what I thought at first, but it's more than that. His character's completely changed just lately. I mean, did you notice how shabby he is? That's not like him. He didn't shave for three days last week, and when I said I didn't think a beard suited him, he got all huffy."

Leigh was puzzled. "He hasn't got a beard."

"He went and shaved, but it looked like he'd done it in the dark. His neck was raw and he had bits of toilet paper stuck on his chin." Owen absently smoothed down his wavy black hair with the palm of his left hand. Leigh recognized the gesture as something he did when he was worried. "There seems to be a problem with his memory too," he added.

"His memory?"

"Yeah. Like, when I was talking to him yesterday, or *trying* to talk to him, I could have sworn he didn't have a clue where Mum was."

"You're kidding!"

"I'm not. He was sort of confused when I mentioned Canada, then he got angry and stormed off. Even when I was a little kid he never lost his temper that badly."

An awkward silence descended. She decided to change the subject. "Did you see them?"

"Hmm?" The question took him by surprise.

She nodded in the direction of the window. "The meteors, or whatever they are."

"Oh. Yeah, I did."

"Why don't we go up to Two Stones Hill tomorrow night? It'd be a great place to watch from if it happens again."

"OK. But I've got to finish the tape for Poppy Morgan first."

"Oh. *Her.*" Leigh made a face. Before Owen could say anything, she added, "They're going to play it then?"

"Well, they *might.* Just 'cause I work there a couple of days a week doesn't mean they're going to like my demo."

Leaning over, she punched his arm playfully. "'Course they will, Owen. It's good!"

"Maybe."

She could see he was distracted and tried to reassure him. "Don't worry about your dad, he's only being cranky."

"Yeah, I expect you're right."

But as he reached over to turn the machine back on he saw the coffee mug, and a shiver tickled his spine.

Owen was jarred awake by a blast of music as his clock radio snapped into life. The red LED numerals winked 07.30 at him. He leaned over, yawning, and whacked the snooze button.

There was a half-full can of diet cola on the bedside table from the night before. He sat up and took a gulp of it to clear the dryness in his mouth. The flat, sticky liquid promptly sand-blasted his taste buds. Grimacing, he slipped out of bed, wriggled into jeans and a sweatshirt, then padded over to draw the curtains.

As he stood blinking at the new day, the radio automatically switched itself on again.

"*. . . watched by a sizeable crowd until the early hours. But experts remain divided about the* *phenomenon. Is it due to meteors? A disintegrating comet? Remnants of a satellite? Perhaps our studio guest can explain the enigma for us."*

Owen seated himself on the bed and listened.

"My name's Mike Adams," the presenter reminded his audience, *"and this is the breakfast show on Radio 525 FM. We're discussing the peculiar goings-on in the skies above Leyswood in the last ten days or so, and..."*

Adams' oily manner was irritating, as usual, but this sounded interesting.

"... I'm joined by Professor Ralph Saul. Professor Saul is an astrophysicist and he's from London, where he acts as an adviser to the Ministry of Defence. Welcome, Ralph."

"Good morning, Mike. Before we go any further, I should explain that I'm here as a private individual, not a representative of the Ministry."

"This isn't an official visit then?"

"No. I had some leave outstanding and simple curiosity brought me here. As far as I'm aware, the MoD hasn't yet made a decision on whether to investigate this particular mystery. Although of course I'd pass on to them any relevant data I might unearth during my stay."

"OK. But as a leading man in your field, what theories do you have about these things? Are they meteors?"

"I don't have a theory as such, but I rather doubt they're meteors."

"Why?"

"Two reasons. First, if the eyewitness accounts are accurate, the objects have been seen travelling parallel to the horizon. Meteors don't do that. Second, no fragments have been found."

"That's significant, is it?"

"Oh, yes. You'd expect to find debris of some sort. And the same applies to falling space hardware. We can forget the idea of a comet, too, because none are known to be in our part of the solar system right now."

"What do you make of the fact that sightings are confined to a radius of approximately six miles around Leyswood?"

"That's another puzzle. It's not unknown for meteor showers to fall in such tight bunches, but as I say, I don't believe these are meteors."

"So what do you hope to achieve during your time here, Ralph?"

"Naturally, I want to observe these objects for myself. Ideally, I'd like to recover one and run a few basic tests on it."

"All right. This is 525 FM and now it's your chance to join the debate. If you have any comments or questions, ring us on..."

Owen finished lacing his trainers and upped the volume a little.

"... and we have someone on the line. His name's Keith and he'd like to speak to the Professor. Go ahead, Keith."

"Uhm, yes." The caller sounded nervous. "I'm convinced we're seeing a massive cover-up by the government and the media. You're all trying to keep the truth from the public."

"What truth?" Saul asked.

"Oh, come on, Professor! I'm talking about secret weapons, of course."

"I beg your pardon?"

"Secret weapons!" Keith was growing heated. "The military's obviously trying out some kind of experimental super-weapon on Leyswood. I think it's outrageous, and as a taxpayer —"

Owen turned off the radio. Listening to the ramblings of a nut suddenly seemed less appealing than the thought of hot coffee. But this time he was going to make it himself.

He went downstairs.

The radio was on in the kitchen. At the far end of the room, apparently engrossed by the broadcast, his father stood with his back to the open door. Keith was still ranting.

"... and I'm sure my headaches are caused by all this radar equipment they're using these days, although heaven knows..."

"Morning, Dad."

His father spun to face him. He moved so quickly,

and the look he wore was so furious, that Owen froze, slightly shocked. Without taking his eyes off his son, Stewart Carter reached over and silenced the radio. For what seemed much longer than the few seconds that actually passed, they stared at each other.

Then Owen said, "Sorry I startled you, I just —"

The apology was cut short by an impatient sweep of his father's hand.

"Don't . . . *creep up* on me . . . that way." He spoke slowly and deliberately, giving the impression he chose his words with care.

"I wasn't, Dad. All I wanted —"

"And don't argue!"

Anger reddened Owen's cheeks. "That's not fair! You won't talk to me, you're in a mood all the time; what have I done?"

The outburst was ignored. His father simply announced, "I have things to do," and walked out.

A flush of hatred ran through Owen, followed by guilt at feeling that way about his own parent. He hefted the kettle, realized he was shaking with suppressed rage, and banged it down again. Taking a deep, calming breath, he forced himself to think logically about what was happening. The most likely explanation was that something must be worrying his dad. Maybe it had to do with money or his job at the university. As Mum wasn't around to share the problem, Owen had to get him to talk about it. Then they could sort things out together.

Couldn't they?

He tried working on the tape, but kept fretting about his father. After an hour he gave up and decided to call on Leigh. Her aunt and uncle's place was nearby, and it was a fine, warm day. The walk lifted Owen's spirits, and by the time he reached their street most of the anger had gone.

Someone was sitting on the garden wall outside the Pearces' house. Drawing closer, he realized it was Eric, Leigh's younger brother.

Eric wore a baggy T-shirt with the word *Chaos* across his chest in huge white print. His battered sunglasses were held together with sticking plaster, his jeans had more patches than denim and one shoe was unlaced. He had his face in a multi-flavour ice-cream so large Owen wondered how he found the strength to lift it.

"'Lo, Eric."

Noticing Owen for the first time, Eric disentangled himself from the cornet and said, "Mumph!" He swallowed and tried again. "Hi, Owen!" Another gulp. "What's happening?"

"Not much. Is Leigh in?"

"Round the shops. Be back in a minute." He renewed his attack on the ice-cream.

"So, what've you been up to?"

Eric grabbed a handful of T-shirt and wiped his mouth with it. Owen winced. "Zero," Eric replied. "I'm bored."

"A week into the summer holidays and you're bored already?"

"Well, nothing ever happens in Leyswood, does it?"

"There's a lot happening *above* it at the moment," Owen said.

"*Yeah!*" Eric brightened. "Leigh said you're going up to Two Stones Hill tonight. Can I come?"

"Well..."

"'Course, if you an' Leigh are just goin' to be snogging all the time, forget it."

Owen smiled. "If it's all right with her, I don't mind you coming. How are you getting on with Aunt Alice and Uncle George?"

"OK, I suppose, though they've been a bit of a pain lately. Wish we could have gone with Mum and Dad."

"Heard from them?"

"Dad rang last night. The line was really bad, but he told Leigh his regiment's tour of duty'll be over before Christmas."

Owen glanced along the road and saw Leigh approaching, laden with shopping bags. "There she is. Looks like she could use some help."

Eric mumbled, mouth crammed, but stayed where he was. Owen jogged off to meet her.

Catching sight of him, Leigh put down the shopping and rubbed her hands. After exchanging hellos, she said, "Am I glad to see *you*." Looking in her brother's direction, she added, "Considering how darling Eric can't be bothered to shift himself."

"The pair of you are still at war, then?"

"You have to hate your little brother," she grinned, "it's a law of nature. Anyway, what are you doing here?"

He picked up the bags. "I had to get out for a while."

"How's your dad?"

"No better."

"Oh."

"It isn't getting any easier, Leigh, and . . ."

"Owen."

". . . this morning he — "

"*Owen*."

She was gazing at something over his shoulder. He turned around. Eric slumped against the wall with his hands pressed to his face. The ice-cream was a rainbow-coloured smear on the pavement. Four boys, older and bigger than Eric, were moving in on him, fists clenched.

Owen dropped the bags and raced towards them.

As he ran, arms pumping, he gave Eric's attackers the once-over.

He had to single out the gang's leader and deal with him. Owen had always been taught that confrontation was the last resort. But if you couldn't avoid it, go for the largest, meanest-looking member of the group and the others would fall into line.

At least, that was the theory.

Identifying the target was no problem. He was a good four inches taller than the rest and built like a barrel. A greasy ponytail dangled from the back of his cropped, bullet-shaped head. Impossibly broad shoulders strained the seams of his faded leather jacket. Despite his bulk, he was around Owen's age.

His friends, no more than pale imitations of their

ringleader, were nearer Eric's generation. So far, they seemed content to jeer in the background. None of them noticed Owen sprinting in their direction.

Eric was still cradling his head. The chief thug was just a foot away from him, shouting, his raised knuckles looking the size of ripe grapefruits. Owen accelerated and hoped the other theory was true as well. The one about bullies really being cowards.

Then there was no more time for thought.

He crashed heavily into the youth menacing Eric. The teenager staggered backwards and almost fell, his face a picture of stupefied surprise. "*Oi!*"

Owen hadn't really hurt him. It would probably take a plasma cannon to do that. But the object was to dent his confidence, not his body. The important thing now was for Owen to take advantage of the element of surprise.

He moved forward.

Knowing that invading a person's space made them uncomfortable, he didn't stop until he was toe to toe with his winded opponent. Close up, he realized he had a slight edge in terms of height, which was a bonus. Locking eyes with his foe, Owen jabbed him hard in the chest with an index finger. "You want to total somebody, try me!" he exclaimed.

"Get lost! It's nothing to do with you!"

Owen thrust out his finger again. "Wanna *bet?*"

"It's personal!"

"Too bad! I just made it my business!"

"There's *four* of us!"

One of the gang piped up, "Yeah, stay out of this!" But it was a half-hearted threat.

Owen ignored it. Once more, he drove his finger into the ballooning chest, *very* sharply. "This is strictly between you and me, dipstick," he said.

The tough flinched. His mates didn't move. Several long seconds went by in silence. Then the leader broke eye contact and retreated a step, muttering, "I ain't got no argument with you."

"Lay off Eric or *I'll* have one with *you*," Owen warned him.

Someone yelled. They turned and saw Leigh elbowing through the rest of the gang, scattering them. She marched up to the ringleader and bellowed. "Clear off, Collins! And stay away from my brother, you *slob*!" Then she underlined the point with a stinging kick to his shin. Collins yelped, doubled over and clutched his leg. His pals stayed where they were. She swung back her boot, as though to kick him again. He tried to hop away, lost his balance and sprawled on the pavement. Hands on hips, Leigh watched in frosty silence as he scrambled up and limped over to the others.

Collins led his gang off down the street, mouthing curses.

Owen and Leigh rushed to Eric. He was stamping his feet while huffing into the palms of his hands and pressing them to his forehead.

"You OK?" Leigh said, laying a hand on his arm.

"Yeah, I think so," her brother replied.

"Where did he hit you?" Owen asked.

"Hit me?" Eric looked blank. "He didn't *hit* me."

"*What?*" Leigh hissed.

"Well, when I saw him coming, I didn't want to give up the ice-cream, so —"

"So you tried bolting it before they got to you," Leigh interrupted, "and it went straight to your empty head. Typical! You little *pig*! We thought you'd been hurt!"

"Aw, come on, sis! They *would've* hurt me if it hadn't been for you and Owen. You know what Pete Collins is like!"

Owen watched the gang disappear around the corner at the end of the street, and began to laugh.

Leigh scowled at him. "What's *your* problem?"

"Sorry, but I can see the funny side of it now."

She rolled her eyes in exasperation and Owen pulled himself together. "Who is this Collins, anyway?" he wanted to know.

"He used to go to my school," Eric explained. "He was always picking on the younger kids, and he's still doing it now."

Leigh said, "You didn't do anything to provoke him, did you, Eric? One of your little jokes, for instance?"

He was offended. "No! You don't have to do

anything to upset Collins. He's always like a bomb waiting to go off."

"If you have any more trouble with him," Owen said, "let me know about it."

Eric smiled his gratitude. "Thanks, Owen."

"You should thank your sister. She frightened those bozos more than I ever could."

"Yeah. Thanks, Leigh."

"But remember," Owen said, "we humiliated him in front of his friends and he lost face. He might try to even the score. Be careful."

"I will."

"Somebody's going to pinch that shopping if we leave it much longer," Leigh announced. She trotted towards the discarded bags. Owen followed.

As they headed back to the house with them, Leigh remembered the conversation Collins and his pals had cut short. "What were you saying about your dad?"

"Oh, yeah. We had a sort of row this morning. Only it wasn't really a row because you can't argue with somebody who won't talk to you."

"Still giving you the dumb treatment, eh?"

"And some. I dunno, maybe he's sulking about something."

"People get that way, Owen. When I got home from seeing you last night our aunt and uncle weren't exactly what you'd call beams of sunshine either."

"Perhaps it's catching!"

They were back with Eric now. He stopped poking at the blob of melting ice-cream with his shoe tip and said, "What is?"

Leigh propped her bags against the front gate. "Bad moods."

"Like Aunt Alice and Uncle George."

"Yes, and Owen's father."

"That's not like your dad, Owen. He's pretty cool. Being a misery at the moment, is he?" Eric asked.

"Even worse than when he gave up smoking. He was irritable for weeks when he did that. *And* he ate like a horse."

Eric snickered. "What, out in the garden with a nosebag, you mean?"

"Very funny," Leigh said, without a trace of amusement.

Owen looked at his watch. "I should be getting home to finish the tape. I have to deliver it to Poppy Morgan at five."

Eric was impressed. "Are you going to be on her show?"

"Possibly," Owen said. "It depends on whether she goes for the demo. Can we set a time to meet this evening?"

"Yeah," said Eric, "we don't want to leave it too late."

"*We?*" his sister queried.

"I'm coming with you. Owen said it'd be OK."

"*Did* he?" If looks could kill, the one she gave

Owen would have struck him down on the spot. "How very considerate of him."

"I, er, knew you wouldn't mind," Owen said lamely.

"Doesn't look as though I've got much choice, does it?"

"We can take Dad's binoculars," Eric declared.

Leigh sighed. "OK, you can come. But I'm taking charge of the binoculars and you're going to stay out of trouble. Right?"

Eric nodded solemnly.

"We'll say your place at seven, Owen," she continued. "It's nearer the moor."

"Fine by me."

Their chat was ended by the arrival of a battered Volkswagen estate car. Leigh and Eric's uncle sat in the driving seat, his wife beside him. The engine cut and they stepped out. Uncle George was a well-built man with thinning hair. He wore a crumpled blue suit. Aunt Alice, a mousy, thin redhead, was dressed in an orange, floral-patterned summer frock. Neither seemed very happy.

"Hi!" Eric and Leigh chorused.

No reply.

"Hello, Mr and Mrs Pearce."

They looked through Owen.

George Pearce reached the gate first. It was blocked by the shopping. Aunt Alice caught up with him. The couple stared at the bags as though they'd never seen anything like them before, and seemed at a loss to know how to handle the situation. Owen had the absurd thought that if he didn't do something everybody would stand there for the rest of the day.

He said, "Let me," and dragged the plastic carriers to one side.

The Pearces swept past him, eyes fixed straight ahead, and hurried along the garden path. They let themselves in and slammed the door behind them.

"See what I mean?" Leigh said.

Owen considered the possibility that everyone had gone mad.

What passed for Leyswood's rush hour was just starting in the town centre. The clock outside the concrete and glass building that housed Radio 525 read 16.51. Owen was early. And nervous. This wasn't like going in on odd days and acting as a studio dogsbody, as he had for the past six months. Today, the station's top DJ had promised to hear his tape, and to make a decision about using it on air. For the twentieth time he patted the jacket pocket containing his demo.

There was a chemist's a couple of doors away. He checked his reflection in its window, smoothing down stray locks of hair with a palm; then he wandered to a video shop to survey its offerings, but without really taking them in.

His house had been empty when he got back from Leigh's, and to be honest, he was glad. Not having Dad creeping around meant he could concentrate on the music.

Owen slapped his pocket again, then glanced over at the clock as it clicked to 16.57, and decided to go in.

525's studios were in the basement. As he came out of the lift, the receptionist greeted him and picked up an internal phone. Seconds later, Poppy bustled through a door, arms laden with CDs and tapes.

Her short, almost delicate build made the load appear even larger than it was. She seemed just as energetic and bubbly as ever, a dynamic sort of person who did everything on the run. Owen liked her, and knew she liked him, too. He felt a little uneasy at the thought that Leigh sometimes had a problem with that.

Poppy's raven black hair was plaited with brightly coloured beads. Several strands hung over her eyes, and they clacked together as she flicked them aside with a toss of her head. There was real warmth in her dazzling white-toothed smile. "Hi, Owen. Like to come through?"

She led him along a corridor to her tiny office. It was a confused jumble, every available surface piled with assorted clutter. Unable to find anywhere else for them, she dumped the tapes and discs on the floor. They spent a moment clearing the chairs of yet more litter and sat down on either side of her desk.

Poppy shoved aside a pile of books. "So, how have you been?"

"Fine, thanks."

"You've brought the demo?"

"'Course," he grinned.

"Yeah, silly of me. I must say you really are persistent in trying to get us to play it." She noted his expression and laughed. "Don't look so worried, that isn't a criticism. You have to be pushy to get anywhere in this business."

Owen relaxed.

"Let's have it then," Poppy said. He pulled out the tape and handed it to her.

Her office had one of the best sound systems Owen had ever seen, including a pair of speakers that nearly reached the low ceiling. She pushed his cassette into the slot and thumbed the play button. The room throbbed with music so loud he felt as much as heard it. It was strange to hear his work coming from someone else's stereo, but he had to admit it sounded pretty good. It looked as though Poppy thought so, too. She was nodding to the complex interwoven beats that backed Owen's wailing keyboard melody. During a quieter passage she mouthed, "*Killer rhythm!*" at him and began drumming on the table top. They listened for about ten minutes. Then Poppy shut off the tape. "Haven't got time for all of it now," she said. "But what I've heard, I like."

"Great!"

"It's put together professionally," she went on, "and there's a richness to it."

Owen beamed.

"You've also avoided the trap of making it all sound the same, which a lot of people don't manage." She leaned back in her chair. "You know, I *love* music, particularly techno stuff like this; but my thing's listening, not producing. Tell me a bit about how you do it. Nothing too deep though."

"Well, it's all done with a synthesizer, coupled to a MIDI."

"Remind me what that is."

"It stands for Musical Instrument Digital Interface. Basically, it means your computer drives a bunch of boxes that actually produce the sounds."

"How do you compose?"

"There's lots of programs for that. I bought an off-the-shelf one and customized it."

"Smart."

He felt himself blushing. "It's easy once you get the hang of it."

"Whatever. I'm impressed."

"Does that mean you'll be using any of it? On tomorrow's show maybe?"

"Probably. But not tomorrow."

Owen's face fell.

"Come on," she told him, "you've hung around here long enough to know how it works. You have to wait your turn."

"OK, Poppy." He trusted her, and knew she'd do her best for him.

"How far do you intend taking the music, Owen? I mean, do you want to make a career of it?"

"I'd like to. My ambition's to get a recording contract."

"You're not alone in *that*. But it can happen. Just keep pushing." She sifted through the mounds of guff on her desk and fished out a small piece of paper. "Do you go to any live gigs?"

"Sometimes."

"I've got a freebie ticket here for one tonight at the community centre. Your sort of stuff. Electronic. Fancy coming along with me?"

"Thanks, but I've arranged to meet some friends."

"Oh." She paused, then said, "Including that girl you know, I suppose. What was her name?"

Owen felt sure Poppy already knew the answer to that question. "Leigh. Yes, she'll be there."

"So you're an item then?" It was said a little too casually.

"Er, yeah, we are." He was uncomfortable at the direction the conversation had taken. "Have been for quite a while."

"Pity." She looked disappointed. "About the ticket," she added quickly, her smile returning. "But let's call it a raincheck. I mean, circumstances change, don't they?"

"Well, I..." Suddenly self-conscious, he was lost for words. Because, in truth, he *did* find Poppy attractive, and for a moment his loyalty was stretched.

She noticed his embarrassment and changed the subject. "Doing anything interesting?"

"Pardon?"

"Tonight."

"Oh, right. We're going up Two Stones Hill to watch the show."

"The mysterious flying circus, eh? What do you think they are?"

"Beats me. Perhaps —"

Her telephone rang. Excusing herself, she lifted the handset. "Poppy Morgan. Oh, hi." A pause. "Yes, I think we can – Hello? *Hello?*" She held the receiver at arm's length and gave it a shake. It hissed and crackled loudly, and she slammed it back into its cradle.

"Blasted phones. Been doing that all week."

"Yeah, I'd noticed," Owen said.

"There's a rumour it's to do with the meteor thingies."

"Can't see how. Particularly if it happens when they're not actually flying around."

"Heard about this Professor Saul guy?"

"I caught him on Mike Adams' show this morning."

"Right. I met him afterwards. He's nice. And *very*

sharp. Anyway, he mentioned the telephones, but couldn't see a connection with these firework displays. He said the only possibility was that if they *were* meteors they might contain deposits of nickel or iron or something, which could interfere with phone lines. Didn't think it was very likely though."

"Another puzzle."

"You said it." She stood up. "OK, I've got to get on. Thanks for coming in. I'll let you know when we'll be using the tape." Her deep brown eyes met his. "And don't forget, if you feel like catching a gig sometime..."

He just smiled, and turned for the door. Opening it for him, Poppy happened to look down the corridor. She quickly ducked back in. "Oh, no!"

"What is it?"

"Ross Waverley, our new owner," she said warily. "You must know about him."

"I know he's a businessman, and that he seems to have bought up half of Leyswood."

"Yeah, he's becoming a real local bigwig. Fingers in every pie."

"What's wrong with him?"

"You obviously haven't had the dubious pleasure of running into him yet. He's a pain in the unmentionable. We're talking major league nasty. But I didn't say that."

Owen grinned. "No, of course you didn't."

Poppy held up her hands, fingers crossed. "With a bit of luck, he won't want to see me today."

Her luck was out. The door opened and an imposing figure strutted in. Middle-aged and around six feet in height, he wore an expensive, tailor-made suit. He had what looked like a fake tan, and immaculate silver-grey hair that seemed equally artificial. Hatchet-faced, eyes burning with single-minded purpose, he radiated an air of arrogant confidence. Waverley had the kind of personality that overwhelmed people. He wasted no time on niceties. "I want to talk to you, Morgan," he boomed.

"Certainly, Mr Waverley." She put as much acid into her voice as she dared. "I was just seeing this young man out."

"He can do that himself."

It was as though Owen wasn't there. A feeling he'd got quite used to recently. He sent a supportive look in Poppy's direction and said, "Thanks for seeing me. 'Bye."

"My pleasure, Owen. So long."

Owen closed the door quietly behind him and was grateful Poppy hadn't tried introducing him to Waverley. No doubt he would have been snubbed. What a *creep* the man was.

There was a black stretch limo with smoked windows parked in the street outside the entrance. Big, showy and pretentious. It was bound to belong to Waverley. A uniformed and capped chauffeur stood beside it, ramrod-straight, arms folded in front of him. As he passed, the driver regarded him with contempt.

Yep, Owen thought, *it had to be Waverley's.*

The house was as welcoming as a morgue. Owen's father was sitting in the living room with the lights out. They did little more than swap grunts, and there was no reaction to the news that Owen's music might be played on the radio. But he could at least draw some comfort from the fact that his dad looked a little more like his old self. He was clean-shaven and his clothes were nowhere near as dishevelled as they had been recently. Maybe that was a good sign.

Owen had just finished changing when the doorbell chimed. It was only ten past six, and Leigh and Eric weren't due until seven. But when he went down he found them standing on the doorstep. Eric looked as buoyant as usual. Leigh, a bulky binoculars case hanging from one shoulder, seemed less cheerful.

Settled in Owen's room, he asked why they were early.

"Couldn't get out fast enough," Leigh said. "The atmosphere's unbearable."

Eric stopped bouncing around on the bed long enough to echo, "Un*bearable*." He started bobbing up and down again. Leigh glared at him and he stopped.

"Our aunt and uncle have been as much fun as scorpions with headaches the last couple of days," she went on. "I'm beginning to see what you're going through with your dad, Owen. I suppose he's still the same?"

"Yeah. No change."

Eric was fiddling with the binoculars. Leigh snatched them away and dropped them into her lap. "Who was it who said, 'You can pick your friends but not your relatives'?"

"I don't know," Owen replied, "but I think they got it about right."

"*Oh!*" Leigh put her hand to her mouth. "Sorry, Owen! I'm so wrapped up in our problem I forgot to ask about ... Poppy Morgan. How did it go?"

He noted her slight hesitation when it came to saying Poppy's name. "She liked the tape, and it's going to be on the show."

"Fantastic!" Leigh said, throwing her arms around him. "When?"

"She wasn't sure, but soon."

"Why don't we play it? We've got time."

While Owen was rummaging for a copy he said, "I met Ross Waverley at 525. Or saw him, rather."

"The entrepreneur?"

"Ontraper*what*?" exclaimed Eric.

Leigh spelled it out for him. "A *businessman*, dummy."

"Oh."

She returned her attention to Owen. "Waverley's got a reputation for being ruthless. How was he?"

"Lived up to his rep, I'd say. Wasn't there a fuss about him in the local paper a couple of months ago?"

"Yeah. He was accused of a shady land deal or something. It blew over."

Owen found the tape. "I feel sorry for Poppy. Now Waverley owns the station I think she's going to have a hard time."

"What a shame." Leigh's tone dripped sarcasm, and her smile evaporated. He almost said something but thought better of it. Instead, he loaded the cassette, and for the next hour they lost themselves in music.

They decided to walk to the moor. It was a pleasant summer evening and still light as they trudged up the rise leading to Two Stones Hill. The nightly event had become a local attraction and lots of other people were moving in the same direction. There must have been a hundred or more spectators milling about on top of the hill. It had a holiday atmosphere. Children ran through the crowd, dogs barked, family groups chattered. Someone had even set up a stall selling fast food, and the smell of fried onions filled the air. Eric spotted a man clutching dozens of silver helium balloons with *I Saw the Leyswood Mystery* printed on them. He pestered Leigh to buy one, but she said it was a waste of money. Then he whined until she gave him enough for a hamburger.

Owen wanted to look at a television outside broadcast van parked on the edge of the throng. They jostled their way towards the camera crew setting up their equipment at its open back doors. Nearby, two journalists interviewed a ginger-bearded, bespectacled man in his late twenties. Owen, Leigh and Eric drifted over and listened.

"... so until we have some hard evidence," the interview subject was saying, "we can't really speculate on the nature of the phenomenon."

One of the reporters scribbled in his notepad and asked, "Do you think there's any danger to the public, Professor Saul?"

That's what Ralph Saul looks like, Owen thought. He had imagined him to be much older.

"There's no reason to believe what's going on

could be harmful," the professor answered. "However, I would caution anyone who comes across anything unusual to contact the authorities. Just to be on the safe side."

"What kind of thing?" the other journalist said, shoving a micro tape recorder at him.

"We don't know at this stage. But it's fair to assume that what's going on is caused by objects of some sort entering the Earth's atmosphere. Whatever they are, it's best to leave them to the experts." He glanced at the setting sun. "Well, gentlemen, if there are no more questions..."

They thanked him and went off to find someone else to interrogate. Owen and the others began moving away too. Then Saul called out, "Excuse me!" and caught up with them.

To Leigh, he said, "I couldn't help noticing your binoculars. This is going to sound a bit cheeky, but is there any chance I could borrow them? I'm a scientist you see, and — "

"You're welcome to share them with us, Professor Saul," she cut in.

"Oh, you know who I am?"

"We just caught the end of your interview."

"And I heard you on the radio this morning," Owen said.

"I stupidly left my own binoculars in the hotel," Saul explained, "so I really would be grateful if you could let me use those."

Leigh smiled and handed him the case. "Sure. They're good."

He examined them. "You're right. And extremely powerful. Military issue, aren't they?"

"Yeah. They belong to my Dad. He's in the army."

Saul put the binoculars back and swung the case on to his shoulder. "Who do I have to thank?"

"I'm Leigh Pearce, this is my brother Eric —"

"Hi, Prof!" Eric broke in.

"— and this is Owen Carter."

"Leigh, Eric, Owen," the professor nodded to each in turn, "pleased to meet you. Are you local?"

Leigh told him they were.

"That could be useful. As a stranger to these parts it would be helpful to have an idea of the general lay-out."

"We'd be glad to show you," Owen offered, pleased at the attention the VIP was paying them. "As a matter of fact, this is probably the best place to do it."

"Excellent! How about a quick geography lesson before it gets dark?"

"No problem." Owen pointed to the top of the hill. "Those are the famous stones."

The two ancient standing stones were no less impressive for the people swarming around their bases. Hewn from bluish rock, and erected thousands of years ago for an unknown purpose by a long-forgotten tribe, the stones stood almost twenty feet in height. They seemed to glow in the dying rays of the sun's red orb, now sinking below the distant horizon.

"Most interesting," Saul observed. "Neolithic, I'd say. Probably as old as Stonehenge."

Owen turned and pointed down the hill at the town, its skyline dominated by the spire of the parish church in the foreground. "Leyswood itself, of course."

"You realize how isolated it is from up here," Saul commented.

"Yes." Owen indicated the surrounding countryside with a sweep of his arm. "Gallows Moor. As you can see, it completely encircles the town."

"A gruesome name," Saul said.

"They used to hang criminals down there, *years* ago," Eric informed him.

Owen could be a bit more precise. "It was the public execution place until the early nineteenth century."

It grew darker by the minute.

"Do you know the moor well, Owen?" Saul asked.

"Pretty well. Leigh and I walk here whenever we can. And my father and I used to come up for motorcycle scrambling. That was a year or two ago."

"Perhaps you heard me say on the radio that I want to find one of these mysterious objects. If there's a chance tonight, will you act as my guide?"

Owen was more than a little flattered. "I'd love to. Can Leigh and Eric come along?"

"Of course." He scanned the growing mass. "But with this mob tramping the moor we might have competition. Something of a zoo, isn't it?"

"There's not much else to do in a place like Leyswood," Leigh said. "And this is the biggest thing that's happened around here for years."

The sky was black now. "Well, at least it's clear," Saul said, "and there's no moon. Perfect conditions for observation."

Then a ripple of excitement ran through the crowd. People craned their necks. A chorus of *ooohs* and *aaahs* arose.

It had begun.

"*There!*"

Eric was the first to spot one. Just above the ragged line that separated land and sky a blazing scarlet blob slit the darkness. It moved rapidly, leaving a thin red streak in its wake before dipping Earthwards and flickering into invisibility. Two more immediately appeared, one slightly higher than the other, zipping right to left over the horizon. They flamed for just a couple of seconds, but the illumination was dazzlingly brilliant.

"Notice how they move," Saul pointed out. "*Across* the sky prior to falling. And look at that!" He indicated a cluster of the things, far to the west, flying left to right. "They don't even travel in the same direction. Remarkable!"

More and more came into view, a spectacular display of flaring pinpoints, each instantly succeeded by another as it died. Soon, the skies teemed with more than the watchers could count.

"Whatever they are," Leigh gasped, "they're *beautiful.*"

"I can't argue with that," Saul agreed, "even if they do defy the laws of physics."

The crowd had grown silent, their chatter replaced by the sound of snapping cameras and whirring camcorders. Owen noted that, for once, Eric seemed lost for words. He stood with his mouth open, head swinging back and forth as though at a tennis match. Owen nudged Leigh. She glanced over and they exchanged grins.

Saul had been trying to follow the objects with the binoculars. He lowered them and said, "They're moving too fast to focus on."

"How far away do you think they are?" Owen asked.

"It's hard to say. We don't know their size, so there's nothing to judge them against. But I'd guess a couple of kilometres."

Owen squinted into the darkness. "Looks to me as though they're roughly over Springfield Mire. That's at *least* two kilometres."

"Well, the reports were right in one way," Saul said.

"How's that?"

"The London taxi syndrome."

"Pardon?" Owen was baffled.

"These objects always seem to come down where people aren't. The same way taxis drive past two streets away from where you're standing."

Owen laughed. "Oh, I get it."

The professor took a folded map and a pen flashlight from his pocket. "That mire's pretty remote, and there's no road near it."

"There are dirt tracks running through. You don't usually find them on a map."

"Could you get us there?"

"Sure."

"My transport's in the lane at the bottom of the hill. Let's go."

"I'm game," Leigh said. "Eric. *Eric!*" She tugged his sleeve. "Come *on*." Her brother snapped back to reality and they began their descent.

On the way down, they were passed by one of the TV people they saw earlier. He was slapping his portable phone and shouting into it, enraged at not being able to get through. Eric thought it quite funny.

A few steps further on he saw something much less amusing.

Pete Collins and his gang were lounging by the hamburger stand. Collins was swigging from a soft drink bottle. His three cohorts were noisily kicking around an empty can and generally making a nuisance of themselves. Owen saw them too. "Don't worry about that bunch,'' he reassured Eric. ''They won't do anything.''

Collins looked over and scowled. Owen stared back at him. Saul noticed what was going on and said, ''Friends of yours?''

''No way!'' Leigh replied, pulling the other two away.

Ralph Saul's vehicle turned out to be a green Range Rover with a white stripe running along its sides. It had a large searchlight bolted to the roof. Owen sat in front with the professor. Leigh and Eric settled in the rear, where she had to help him sort out the mess he got into with his seat-belt. Then Saul gunned the engine and they set off. As they sped along country lanes, deeper into the moor, the mysterious objects continued to shimmer overhead.

''What I don't understand is why these things wait for the dark.'' Leigh addressed the question at Saul's reflection in the rear-view mirror above his head.

''Perhaps they don't,'' he said, crunching gears. ''They could be falling all the time. It has to be dark for us to see them.''

''Of *course*. Silly me.''

Eric smirked. ''Nought out of ten for Leigh.''

''Now that you've seen them, Professor,'' Owen said, ''do you have any better idea what they might be?''

''Not really. In fact, because of the peculiar way

these UFOs behave, I'm more puzzled now than before."

"UFOs?" Eric blurted. "You think they're *flying saucers*, prof?"

"Sorry about my brother," Leigh said. "He's a twerp."

Saul grinned. "It's a common misunderstanding. UFO stands for unidentified flying object, remember. Well, what we have here are unidentified, flying, and presumably objects of some sort. As a scientist I have to keep an open mind, of course, but I don't think little green men come into it."

Eric looked disappointed.

Owen sank in his seat to get a better look at the sky. "There doesn't seem to be so many of them now." He sat up again and added, "The mire's about half a mile from here. Take the second on the left."

The road was not much more than pot-holed earth, and Owen was glad they were in a four-wheeled drive. Even so, it was a rocky ride. After several minutes bumping along the dirt track a small wood loomed on their right-hand side. "It's just beyond this copse," Owen explained. "You should be able to turn off after the trees."

They parked in a clearing. It was eerily quiet. The ground was spongy and damp, despite the summer warmth, and their shoes made sucking noises when they walked on it. Saul turned on the floodlight, sending a powerful yellow shaft through the darkness. He slowly rotated the beam through three hundred and sixty degrees, lighting up the surrounding landscape to a distance of about fifty metres. Then he switched it off.

"This is like cracking a nut with a sledgehammer. We need to check the area more closely." He opened the back of the Range Rover and hunted through the boxes stored there. Finally locating a couple of heavy-duty torches, he handed one to Owen.

"I suggest we form two groups. And if you come across something out of the ordinary, *don't touch it*." Saul produced a small silver whistle and gave that to Owen too. "Blow this if you find anything." He peered at his watch. "We'll set a time limit of, say, thirty minutes."

They agreed that Owen would go with Eric, Leigh with the professor. One pair would search to the right of the vehicle, the other to its left.

As they were about to start, Owen warned, "Don't go too far that way," and pointed further along the track they'd turned off. "It leads to Springfield Mire. You'll find yourselves waist-deep in swamp before you know it."

For the next twenty minutes the two groups edged their way through the moist grass. They investigated rocks, clumps of bark and occasional pieces of litter, but found nothing out of the ordinary.

By now the sky was more serene, disturbed only by a fleeting slash of crimson every few minutes.

Eric and Owen worked their way to the edge of the wood. Owen had the torch and was busy examining a heap of soggy leaves. Eric, the whistle in his mouth, toed an abandoned pizza carton to one side.

A sharp crack came from the depths of the trees. It sounded like someone stepping on a branch. They froze. There was a rustling noise, following by approaching, squelchy footsteps.

Owen brought up the torch and aimed it in the direction of the sounds.

Standing by a tree trunk, no more than ten feet away, was a figure dressed in black.

Eric gaped and the whistle dropped out of his mouth.

The figure, its face shadow-shrouded, took a step towards them. Owen drew back the torch intending to use it as a weapon. The figure moved nearer and started to raise an arm.

A shrill, high-pitched note split the silence.

Owen and Eric jolted in surprise. The torch beam wavered, and darkness enveloped whatever was advancing on them.

The note rang out again, and Owen realized it had to be Saul and Leigh's whistle. He directed the beam back at the trees.

The figure had gone.

They wasted no time getting to the car. The others

were already there. When she noticed the look on Owen's and Eric's faces, Leigh said, "What's the matter with you two?"

"We saw a man, or something, over by the wood," Owen told her. "It gave us a bit of a shock."

"It was *spooky*," Eric declared.

"I expect it was just somebody else trying to find debris, the same as us," the professor suggested.

"Yes," Owen decided, "that must have been it. Did you have any luck?"

"No," said Leigh. "I blew the whistle because the half hour's up."

"I'm glad you did," Eric told her. "You probably saved our lives."

"Trust you to exaggerate," she said. "It's getting late. We should be heading for home."

They piled into the Range Rover. The sky was empty now, and everyone was slightly dispirited at not having found the evidence Saul needed. As they were turning into the road where it met the mud path, they heard another motor.

Suddenly, a jeep shot past them, narrowly missing the front of their vehicle. Saul hit the brakes hard and they were all thrown forward against the seat-belts.

"Idiot!" he grumbled as he got the stalled engine going again. "Some people shouldn't be allowed behind a wheel!"

It had happened very quickly. But for a fraction of a second, as the jeep passed them, Owen caught sight of the driver. There was something familiar about him.

He massaged the bridge of his nose with a thumb and forefinger. It had been a long day and he was tired. Perhaps he just *thought* he recognized the man.

But his face was in Owen's mind all the way home.

Owen woke up thinking about the face. Not being able to place it irritated him. But he'd often found the best way to remember something was to stop *trying* to remember it. So he put the problem to one side.

His father was out when he got back. Presumably he came in some time during the night and Owen hadn't heard him. This morning, his bedroom door was firmly closed, and there was no answer when Owen knocked. He was relieved. Things had been so bad between them lately, he welcomed a rest from his dad's loony toons behaviour.

Now the tape was finished and delivered, Owen was at a loose end. As he wasn't the sort of person to sit around doing nothing, he decided to clean up the house. His father certainly didn't seem to be bothering. Layers of dust covered the furniture in the living room and the carpets needed vacuuming. There were huge piles of dirty crockery in the kitchen sink.

An hour later, as he clacked the last of the wet dishes on the draining board, he heard his father coming down the stairs. Stewart Carter walked past the kitchen, ignoring his son's greeting and let himself out of the house. He slammed the front door with such force the window over the sink rattled in its frame. Owen bit back the increasingly familiar rush of annoyance.

He went to see if there was anything on TV about last night's events. All the channels kept dissolving into white snowstorms of interference, and he couldn't even get clear sound. After ten minutes he gave up and made a note to talk to the rental people about it. Looking for an excuse to get out of the house, he remembered he needed computer disks. He called Leigh to ask if she'd like to go with him. They barely managed to agree on the time and place before the telephone line drowned in static.

She was waiting for him at the shopping parade. Her new denim trouser suit hadn't had a chance to wear smooth yet. But the peaked blue cap of the same material she had on was older and looked slightly shabby by comparison. Not that Owen was likely to tell her that.

"What, no Eric?" he said as he walked over to her.

"I managed to shake him off for once."

"What's he doing?"

"Driving me mad by playing shoot-'em-up computer games. When he isn't complaining about not being able to get the TV to work, that is."

"Funny, ours is on the blink too. The shop where we rent it's along here; mind if we pop in?"

"'Course not. I've got all day. You know, a couple of our neighbours mentioned bad television reception, too. Maybe it's sunspots or something."

They got the disks first. Then, as they walked hand in hand to the television store, the subject of Ralph Saul came up. "I like him," Leigh said. "He was even nice about Eric losing his whistle!"

"Yeah, I liked him as well. Thought he was a bit young though. For a professor, I mean."

"What were you expecting, Albert Einstein?"

Owen chuckled. "After we dropped you and Eric off, he said he was going to request some specialist equipment from London today. Infrared cameras, that kind of stuff. And he gave me the number of his hotel."

"Not much point in that, considering there's only the one," Leigh commented. "Why did he give it to you?"

"Thought we might like to go sky-watching with him again sometime. He said we could call and he'd pick us up."

"Perhaps he was just being polite. You know, for helping him out last night."

"Could be."

The TV shop was surprisingly crowded for a weekday and they had to queue. When they finally got to the counter, they found a flustered young sales assistant sorting heaps of paperwork. "Don't tell me," she said, "let me guess. Your TV's not working properly."

"Got it in one," Owen confirmed. "You must be a mind reader."

"Nope." The girl slid a stick of gum into her mouth. "Everybody's been complaining about it." She pushed a yellow form at him. "Fill this in, please."

Leigh glanced at the assistant's name badge. "My set's up the creek too, Tracy, and . . . "

Tracy started to peel off another form.

"No," Leigh said, "ours isn't rented. I was going to ask if you knew what was going on."

Tracy's vigorous chewing made her pink lips look like two demented worms. "We think it's to do with these whatchamacallits everybody's getting excited about. The meteors. Blocking the signals or whatever it is they do. So it could be the engineers won't be able to help anyway."

Owen handed her the completed form. She added it to the pile and said, "We're rushed off our feet, so don't expect anybody to call soon. Next!"

Outside, the street was growing crowded as people

finished work for the day. Leigh and Owen began wandering, more or less aimlessly. Then they turned a corner and almost collided with a mature, somewhat dowdy woman, wearing a Laura Ashley smock, large straw hat and sensible shoes. It was Grace Harvey, an English teacher from their school. "Oh, sorry!" Leigh exclaimed.

Owen said, "Afternoon, Mrs Harvey."

The woman stared at them. It was not a kind look. The expression on her face was disdainful, and there was no hint of recognition in the void of her eyes.

"Er, it's us, Mrs Harvey. Leigh Pearce and —"

"Kindly leave me alone." The words cut like an ice dagger. Her face a rigid mask, Grace Harvey turned her back on them and disappeared into the crowd.

"Well, she was a barrel of laughs, wasn't she?" Owen said.

"Why did she have to be so *rude*?" Leigh fumed. "She isn't normally like that at all. What's going on in this town, Owen?"

"I don't know. Do you think it could be the heat?"

But it wasn't really funny.

Leigh wasn't keen on going back to her aunt and uncle's until as late as possible. So they decided to listen to Poppy Morgan's show at Owen's house. It was getting dark when they arrived. And Owen's father was still out.

Owen made himself comfortable in his room's

only good chair, with Leigh sitting on his lap. But less than five minutes into the programme the radio was swamped by hissing, pops and crackles. Owen fiddled with it, fussed with its extendible aerial and searched the other channels. All they could get was rasping interference. "Nothing seems to work any more," he complained, and switched off the set.

"At least we know Poppy wasn't going to play your stuff tonight," Leigh said. "Let's have a tape. Can I pick one?"

Owen clicked on a table lamp. "Go ahead. And draw the curtains while you're there, will you?"

She crossed to the window. About to swish the blinds, she paused and stood on tiptoe. Flecks of red splashed the night sky. "Here we go again."

Owen didn't bother moving. "It's almost routine now, isn't it?"

Leigh dropped her gaze to the street below. She was quiet for a moment, arms still stretched to either side, hands clasping the two halves of the curtains.

Then she said, "Owen, come and look at this."

"And turn that light out!"

Owen did as he was told and joined her at the window. Opposite, three or four houses to the right, a car stood with its engine running. It was a black stretch limousine with smoked glass windows.

"I know that car," Owen said.

Leigh put a finger to her lips. "*Ssshhh!*"

They couldn't possibly be heard from such a distance. But there was something about the scene that made Owen lower his voice. "What's happening?"

"See him?" she whispered, pointing beyond the limo.

A figure Owen hadn't noticed stood in the shadow of a tree in the house's front garden. He seemed to be dressed in black.

"Two others went in," Leigh added. "They looked really furtive."

"Burglars?"

"No. Well, they didn't *break* in. But..."

"What?"

"They rang the bell and somebody answered the door. Then..." A doubtful expression played across her face, "... it was hard to tell from here, but there seemed to be some kind of scuffle."

"You mean they forced their way in?"

"I don't know. I mean, the light's not good, is it? I could be wrong."

Apart from the gently purring car and the unmoving figure, the street was deserted.

"Whose house is it?" Leigh asked.

"A man about my dad's age. Lives there by himself. I don't know his name."

The door of the house they were watching opened and indistinct shapes moved along the path. It was too dark to make out what they were. The man by the tree went over and held the gate open. Two other men, dressed identically to the first, shuffled on to the pavement and into the glow of a streetlamp. They were carrying something bulky and about six feet in length, wrapped in what could have been a carpet.

"Are you thinking what I'm thinking?" Owen said.

"A *body*!" Leigh gasped, her eyes like saucers.

The trio had reached the car now, and the first man was opening its boot.

"We have to *do* something," Leigh said.

The men were depositing their load in the back of the limo.

Owen hit the floor and started wriggling under his bed. Leigh was outraged. "Owen! How can you *hide* at a time like this?"

He re-emerged with a cricket bat in his hand. "What was that?"

"Oh. Uhm. Nothing."

"Let's go then!" he shouted, and headed for the door.

By the time they got outside, the car was gliding away. They ran after it, but it picked up speed and screeched around the corner. "Did you get the number?" Leigh panted.

"No. I think it might have been covered up."

"Let's call the police." She eyed the cricket bat. "And do get rid of that stupid thing."

In the house, Owen snatched up the hall telephone and punched three nines. "*Come on!*" he cried, and rattled the receiver. He jabbed the number again, glared, and smacked the phone back into its cradle. "Would you believe it! I can't get through. More blasted interference!"

"Let me try." Leigh took the phone and carefully dialled triple nine. There was nothing but white noise. "You're right. We'll have to go round to the police station."

The sky flashed with red mysteries as they hurried along the street.

The burly sergeant slowly flipped the pages of the massive ledger on his desk. "I'm sure I've seen you two before. What did you say your names were?"

Leigh was annoyed at the policeman's lack of urgency. "Must we go through all that again?" she said. "We've just witnessed a murder or a kidnapping or something, and you're —"

"We have to follow procedure," the sergeant informed her sternly. "Names?"

Sighing, Owen recited, "Owen Carter and Leigh Pearce."

The sergeant carefully wrote the information in his ledger. "Addresses?" Owen gave them to him.

"Address where you say the incident took place?" Owen gave him that too.

"Where are your parents?" Owen explained, and watched with mounting irritation as the sergeant painstakingly entered his answer.

"Ever been in trouble with the police?"

"*What?*" Leigh exclaimed. "We're here to report a crime, not confess to one!"

"No," Owen interjected. "We've never been in trouble with the police."

Another half minute passed as the sergeant's pen leisurely moved across the page. Then he looked up and said, "Now tell me exactly what you think you saw."

"This is ridiculous," Leigh fumed. "Why don't you —"

"*If* you don't mind, miss, I'm asking the questions here. Calm yourselves and give me the details." He turned to a fresh page in the ledger.

"About an hour ago," Owen explained, "we saw three men behaving suspiciously in my street. They came out of a neighbour's house and drove off with what looked like a body."

"*Looked* like a body?"

"We couldn't be sure. It was wrapped in something."

"I see. And you say you don't know the name of this neighbour?"

"No."

"Just a minute." The sergeant scribbled on a piece of paper, then pressed a button on the intercom beside him. "Come in here, would you, Andrews?"

A young poker-faced constable barged through the door on the far side of the room. He looked at Owen and Leigh as though he'd just scraped them off his shoe. Handing the sheet of paper to him, the sergeant said, "Find out who lives at this address and see if you can get in touch with them. I want to know if anything out of the ordinary happened there tonight."

"Yes, Sergeant."

As Andrews left, the sergeant resumed his questioning. "Give me a description of these men."

"We didn't get a good look at them," Leigh admitted, "but they were all dressed the same way, in black."

"'Dressed in black,'" the policeman repeated as he wrote it down. "And their vehicle?"

Owen took over. "A black stretch limousine. We didn't get the number, but I've seen it before. It belongs to Ross Waverley."

The sergeant put his pen down. "The businessman? How do you know it was his car?"

"I don't actually *know* it's his, but I saw it parked outside the —"

"Let's get this straight. You're saying three men you can't really describe did something you couldn't see properly. And they were driving a car you didn't get the number of, but you *think* it belongs to Ross Waverley. Does that sum it up?"

"Well, if you put it that way —" Owen began.

"Mr Waverley's a highly respected member of this community. I'd be very careful about slander if I were you, young man."

"*Slander?* Look, we saw —"

The sergeant interrupted again. "The most likely explanation is that you and your girlfriend saw some perfectly normal event and let your imaginations get the better of you, being —"

"*Perfectly normal?*" Leigh raged. "There was nothing normal about —"

"—being of a somewhat excitable nature," the sergeant finished smugly.

"That's unfair," Owen protested. "We wouldn't have come here if —"

The door banged. Constable Andrews reappeared, a notebook in his hand. His mood seemed no brighter. "Well?" his sergeant asked.

Andrews consulted the pad. "The occupant of that address is a Mr Turner. He works for the electricity company."

"And?"

"I spoke to him on the telephone," Andrews continued tonelessly, "and he said nothing unusual had occurred. He did mention that some friends were there earlier helping him move items of furniture."

"In a *limousine?*" Owen said.

The constable glared at him.

"All right. Thank you, Andrews." The sergeant took his pen and ran a stroke through the page he'd written. He addressed Leigh and Owen frostily. "I'll give you two the benefit of the doubt. But if you try wasting police time again, I'll come down on you like a tonne of bricks. Now get yourselves home!"

Outside the police station, Leigh was nearly speechless with anger. "How *dare* he accuse us of making it up!"

"He wasn't exactly helpful."

"We weren't wrong, were we, Owen? I mean, there *was* something strange going on, wasn't there?"

"*I* thought so. But they say this Turner guy's OK, so ... what else can we do?"

"'Benefit of the doubt' indeed," she grumbled.

"I suppose they know what they're doing. At least they can get *their* telephones to work."

"Yes," Leigh said thoughtfully, "they can, can't they?"

"What I find really suspicious is the limousine," Owen said. "How many cars like that can there be in Leyswood?"

"Shouldn't think there's more than one."

They were approaching the entrance to the park. If it was still open they could take a short-cut to Leigh's aunt and uncle's. "But let's face it," she went on, "that dope of a sergeant must have been right. We blew it."

"Maybe. I doubt it though."

"What other explanation is there?"

"It could be the police got it wrong. They only made a phone call. How do they know who it was that answered?"

"Hadn't thought of that." She turned her collar up

against a slight chill in the air. "There's another possibility, Owen. They might have been lying to us."

"Yeah, I know. But why?"

"Search me."

The park gates were fastened with a heavy padlock and chain. Owen rattled them. "Trust our luck. That's another twenty minutes while we go the long way round."

"We don't have to," Leigh said, reaching for a handhold. She was half-way up, with Owen about to follow, when a car horn gave three short toots behind them. To their relief, Professor Saul's Range Rover drew level.

He poked his head out of the window and called, "Like a lift?"

Owen expelled the breath he'd been holding and steadied the gate while Leigh climbed down again. Saul regarded them with amusement as they got in the back of his car and gave him directions. "Dare I ask what you were doing?" he said as they moved off.

Leigh snuggled up to Owen and grinned. "Nothing awful. Just trying to avoid a long walk home."

"Good thing I came along. What have you two been up to?"

They told him about the bizarre scene they'd witnessed, and how the police reacted. Saul listened patiently, then said, "You know, science is mostly observation, and it teaches you that things aren't always what they seem to be."

"So you think we were mistaken?" Leigh asked.

"Not necessarily. Science also demonstrates how valid that famous Sherlock Holmes quote is. The one that says when you've eliminated the probable, whatever's left, no matter how improbable, must be the truth. Your story's improbable enough to be true."

Owen said, "I don't quite understand."

"I'm thinking of that limousine," Saul explained. "If you'd made up the story –" He saw the look on Leigh's face and hurriedly added, "– not that I believe you did, of course, but if you *had*, why include an unusual car belonging to a local celebrity? It's too easily disproved."

"But the police *didn't* disprove it," Owen insisted. "At least, they didn't say anything about checking with Ross Waverley."

"In which case they were at fault," Saul said. "Then again, perhaps your neighbour's a friend of Waverley's. That would explain his car being there."

"Could be. But I can't see him letting it be used to move furniture."

"Neither can I. And I find it even harder to believe Waverley *has* any friends."

"Oh, you've met him too," Owen chuckled.

"At the radio station. And I wouldn't put anything past that particularly unpleasant gentleman."

They halted at a set of traffic lights. "That reminds

me," Owen said. "Poppy Morgan mentioned talking to you about the phones not working properly."

"Ah, you know Ms Morgan. This *is* a small town."

At the mention of Poppy's name, Leigh directed a mildly accusing glance Owen's way. The lights turned green and they carried on.

"Of course, it isn't just the telephones now," Saul continued. "Have you noticed how bad radio and TV reception is? And it's getting worse. I tried sending a fax this morning, to chase the equipment I requested from London, and *that* wasn't working either. Are there any radio hams in Leyswood, Owen?"

"Not that I know of."

"Pity. I'd be interested in whether they're affected too."

"Do you think this is all connected with the so-called meteors, Professor?" Leigh said.

"There's no logical reason it should be. Even if these things *are* meteors, and I'm sure they're not, they wouldn't interfere with phone lines and broadcast signals. It's never been known. But as a scientist I have to work on the evidence."

"You mean there *is* a connection?"

"We can't ignore the fact that these unidentified objects are manifesting at the same time as a breakdown of communications. It's starting to look too much of a coincidence."

"But you can't see a direct link," Owen suggested.

"Exactly." Saul grew reflective. "It's not the only

thing nagging at me, though. I've given a lot of thought to what's happening in Leyswood, and I'm beginning to develop . . . well, it's too early to call it a theory. And there were fewer people on the hill tonight. That could be significant."

"In what way?"

"I'd rather not go into it at the moment, Owen." His eyes took on a bright intensity. "But if I'm right, what's going on here is truly . . ." He shook his head. "No, it's too soon. I need to think this through." He noted their puzzlement and smiled wryly, adding, "Let's just say that, like Sherlock Holmes, I'm being forced to consider the improbable."

Owen and Leigh wanted to ask more, but they'd arrived at George and Alice Pearce's house. As Leigh walked to the front door, Owen chanced to look up. Although the windows on the first floor were in darkness, he could just make out her aunt and uncle at one of them, staring down at the Range Rover. They were motionless, their pallid faces lacking any kind of expression. Owen understood their concern about their niece getting home safely. So why did he feel such discomfort at their unblinking gaze?

Ralph Saul seemed preoccupied as he drove Owen home, and the journey passed in near silence.

Owen wondered if he was doing the right thing.

It was near midnight and there were no lights on in the house. Owen hesitated at the door. Perhaps he should come back in the morning. His neighbour was hardly likely to thank him for being dragged out of bed at this hour. Anyway, what was Owen going to say to him?

But his curiosity was too strong to let him walk away. Something unusual had happened here tonight, he was sure of it. And he didn't buy the police version. Assuming they *had* rung this man Turner, how did they know someone wasn't impersonating him? Whereas Owen had seen him lots of times and knew what he looked like.

He took a deep breath and pressed the doorbell.

The chimes sounded horribly loud. But after they faded, the house remained silent. Owen counted to fifty in his head and tried again. Nothing happened. There was no noise or sign of movement inside, yet he had the distinct impression someone was in. It was the same feeling he got when he walked into a darkened room and knew somebody else was there.

Owen thumbed the bell for the last time, waited a few seconds and started to leave.

A tiny clink of metal on metal stopped him in his tracks.

He turned to see the door creaking open a few inches. Someone peered at him through the gap. The hallway was unlit, but as far as he could tell, the man looked like his neighbour. He was short and muscular, with an oval face and almost completely bald dome. His expression was grim.

"Er, Mr Turner?"

Turner could have been a shop window dummy for all the reaction Owen got.

"I'm sorry to disturb you so late..." He almost faltered. "... but I live across the road, and —"

"No."

It seemed such an odd thing to say that Owen thought he must have misheard. He leaned closer. The smell of stale tobacco filled his nostrils.

"I beg your —"

"*No*," Turner repeated, his voice as rough as sandpaper on gravel. "Not wanted. Mind your ... business. Go away!"

Owen found himself staring at the closed door. "Well, thanks very much, Mr Turner," he told it sarcastically. "Enjoyed our chat. We must do it again sometime."

Trudging off, he thought about the peculiar way Turner spoke, and how he seemed to struggle for the right words. Owen added it to the growing list of bizarre incidents plaguing Leyswood; another piece in the jigsaw of a mystery he couldn't begin to grasp. He didn't want to think about it now. All he wanted was to sleep.

His own house was in darkness. The last thing he needed was a run-in with his father. He was probably out, as he often had been recently, or in bed. But Owen wasn't taking any chances. Quietly closing the gate, he crept along the path, key at the ready.

The lock turned smoothly.

He slowly edged the door open, just far enough to let him slip in and ease it shut behind him. Ignoring the light switch, he padded to the foot of the stairs, intending to take off his shoes before climbing to his room.

Then he had that feeling again. The prickle at the back of his neck that told him he wasn't alone. He couldn't see or hear anything, but he *knew* someone was concealed in the pool of surrounding blackness. If it was his dad, wouldn't he speak?

A vivid picture came to mind. A scene of black-garbed men slinking through the night, trussed bodies and sinister limousines.

He had a couple of choices. He could try running up the stairs. He could head for the living room or kitchen, both of which were off the hall. Or he could get himself back into the street. The street seemed the best option.

Owen fought hard not to panic. Then he steeled himself, tensed his muscles and rushed for the front door.

He thought he was going to make it.

Until someone stepped out of the shadows and snapped on the light.

Stewart Carter stood in front of the door, one hand on the light switch. Owen's shock gave way to relief. Followed by anger.

"*Hell*, Dad, you gave me a fright! What were you doing hiding in the dark like that?"

His father didn't answer. Then Owen became aware of the poisonous look on his face. And of his eyes, intense and ill-tempered behind their thick bifocals. Owen experienced a twinge of fear. It was the first time in his life his father had made him feel that way.

"Look," he said, "don't you think we should —"

"*Listen to me!*" The force of the command stopped Owen in his tracks. His father slapped his right index finger on his left palm. "You have been bothering a neighbour. This will stop." Two fingers came down on the open palm. "You will not talk to the police." Three fingers and another sharp thwack. "You will stay away from Ralph Saul."

That did it. Owen wasn't taking a shopping list of demands. Nor would he back down before a man who seemed like a stranger to him now.

"I've not been *bothering* anyone!" he retorted. "I suppose the police have been talking to you. I don't know what they said, but —"

"You had no business involving them."

"I went to them because I thought it was the right thing to do, can't you understand that? And as far as Professor Saul's concerned —"

"The man is a bad influence. You will not see him again."

"A bad...?" Owen's rage mounted. "This is *crazy*! You're saying I can't talk to anyone or hang out with people you don't approve of. What is this, a prison?"

Stewart Carter moved towards his son. He did it unhurriedly, which somehow added to the menace he radiated. His fists were tightly clenched. "You will do as you are told. You will obey me."

"*Obey* you! You're a dictator now, is that it?"

With startling speed his father darted forward and grabbed Owen's wrist. Owen tried to pull away, but the grip was like an iron band. He found himself staring into piercing, flinty eyes. "*You will do as I say.*"

"You sound like a blasted robot, Dad! *Let go!*"

Owen struggled harder. But the hold was unbreakable. In desperation he hit out with his free hand, and swiped only air. He swung his fist a second time and struck his father's glasses. They flew off and clattered along the hall floor. Without the powerful spectacles he was temporarily blinded. Owen seized the opportunity to twist free.

But he couldn't get to the front door. His father was moving that way in search of the glasses, a hand on the wall to guide him, feet shuffling. Owen hurtled into the living room and slammed the door. There was no key in the lock so he dragged over a chair and wedged it under the handle.

Almost immediately the handle turned. He threw himself into the chair and pushed all of his weight against the door. A frenzied pounding hammered at it. And as abruptly stopped.

Owen was shaking. He pressed his ear to the door. It was quiet outside. A minute passed in complete silence. Then another. He relaxed a little. Now what?

Scanning the room, his eye fell upon the telephone. He thought of calling the police, but dismissed the idea. They probably wouldn't believe him again. Or they'd take his dad's side. No, the only person likely to understand was Leigh. Assuming she was still up, and that the telephone was working.

He was surprised to get a clear dialling tone. And the number rang only twice before Leigh answered.

She sounded worried herself, and said she had been thinking about ringing *him*. Then she caught the tension in his voice and asked what was wrong.

"I'm having a really bad time with my father. The worst yet." He filled her in on the night's events and finished with, "If he's starting to get violent I don't want to be here."

"That's incredible. *I've* just had a row with my aunt and uncle, and it sounds like they were using the same script. Don't talk to the police, stay away from Ralph Saul, all that stuff. Though they didn't get as rough as your dad."

"Quite a coincidence, eh?"

"You said it."

"What are we going to do?"

"Well, things are pretty grim here, so I was going to go home and spend the night there. Why don't you come? There's plenty of room."

"Thanks, Leigh, I think I will. What about Eric?"

"He's in bed, and I don't think he heard any of it. But he'll be OK, it was me they were giving the treatment. I'll check on him tomorrow."

The line began to crackle. "I thought this was too good to be true," Owen said. "I'm leaving now. See you at your mum and dad's."

As he was about to replace the phone he heard a loud click, and he didn't think it was interference. It sounded like someone putting down an extension. His father? Leigh's aunt or uncle? Frowning, Owen thought about how to get out of the house without having to face his dad. He glanced at the door and wondered if it was safe to risk using it. Then realized he didn't have to.

He unlatched the living room window, raised it and eased himself over the sill.

Owen and Leigh sat in the kitchen of her parents' flat drinking coffee.

And the world slept.

Leigh put down her cup and said, "How are you feeling?"

"A couple of hours ago I would have said I was dead tired. But it's funny how being insulted, attacked and made homeless tends to wake you up."

She grinned. "Fool."

He reached for the coffee pot and poured himself a refill. "Are you serious about moving back here?"

"Yes. And I'm bringing Eric with me. I've had enough of living with the relatives from hell."

"But aren't they your guardians or something while your parents are away?"

"Kind of. But I thought if I could explain things to Dad, he'd say it was OK. Only I tried ringing Saudi earlier and couldn't get through."

"The good old phone system again."

"Right. I'll have another go tomorrow." She looked at the clock on the wall. "Or later today, rather. You could stay here for a while too, Owen, until things sort themselves out."

"I can't see my psycho father going for that one."

"It'd just be for a couple of weeks. Then your mother will be back and so will my parents."

"I dunno. Let's talk about it later."

"Sure. You'll see it differently after some sleep." She got up. "But first, there's something you can help me with. Come on."

He followed her upstairs and into the spare room at the end of the landing. It was piled high with old furniture and bric-a-brac. Leigh went to a battered wardrobe and took out a bundle wrapped in brown cloth, smelling faintly of oil. "I want this put where Eric won't find it. Any ideas?" She handed the package to Owen and he unwrapped it.

There was a gun inside.

He was stunned. A revolver was the last thing he had expected to see.

"It's all right," Leigh assured him, "it's not loaded." She rattled a small orange and white box. "The bullets are in here. Forty-five calibre."

Weighing the pistol in his hand, Owen noted it felt much heavier than it looked. "I can see why you wouldn't want Eric getting hold of *this*."

"You said it." She laughed. "I have visions of Pete Collins never being able to sit down again."

"It must be your dad's, yeah?"

"It's a souvenir. Quite old. A Webley 455 service

revolver, to be exact. He thought it'd be safe to leave it here, with Eric not around. But if he's coming back it's got to be hidden."

Owen held the weapon at arm's length and squinted along its sights.

"Don't play around with it," Leigh said, "it makes me nervous. I *hate* guns."

"Sorry." He lowered it.

"So where do we hide the thing?"

"Good question."

He looked around the room and noticed a metal grille, about the size of a letterbox, set high in the opposite wall. "What's that?" he asked.

"An air vent."

"Perfect. I'll take the cover off and put it in there." He began winding the cloth around the revolver and its box of shells. "Got a screwdriver?"

"I don't think so."

"Not to worry, I can use a coin."

The doorbell rang. "Who can that be at this time of night?" Owen wondered.

"It's got to be my aunt and uncle, hasn't it?" Leigh sighed. "You stay here. And prepare yourself for a row." She scooted off.

Owen decided to finish the job, and carried a chair over to the vent.

He had one foot on it when an ear-splitting scream rang out downstairs.

Owen kicked away the chair and raced from the room. He yelled, *"Leigh!"* There was no answer.

Taking the stairs three at a time, he leapt the last half dozen, hitting the first-floor landing hard. As he reached the top of the flight leading down to the front door another scream sounded. But it was suddenly muffled.

The hallway below was a well of darkness.

He could just make out two struggling figures. The nearest had the same build as Leigh. The other was tall and much broader. Owen knew there was a light switch nearby. Frantically, he groped along the wall to find it.

When he snapped it on, the scene was shocking.

Leigh wriggled in the clutches of a man dressed in black. He wore a balaclava, with eye holes cut in it, and had a gloved hand clamped over her mouth.

The light caught her attacker by surprise and Leigh took advantage of the diversion to wrench an arm free. Then she drove her elbow into his ribcage with all her strength. It was enough to throw him off balance, and he spiralled to one side, releasing his grip. Leigh staggered a couple of paces and collapsed.

Owen had been transfixed, rooted to the spot as though in a trance. Now he acted.

He charged down the stairs. But before he got to ground level the intruder was moving towards Leigh again. Owen launched into a diving tackle, hitting the man at waist height. The bone-jarring impact sent him crashing against a full-length mirror on the wall. It shattered and he went down in a hail of broken shards.

Leigh was on her feet, looking dazed. Owen backed away from the fallen man, grabbed her hand and shouted, "Quick!"

He pulled her to the front door. They yanked it open. And faced another man in black.

They tried to shut him out, pushing as hard as they could. It was like leaning into a hurricane. Slowly but steadily the door gave inwards.

"It's no use, Owen!"

"Upstairs!"

As the door burst open they turned and ran, crunching over pieces of mirror. The first man was on his hands and knees, shedding glass fragments. He swiped at Owen's leg and missed. Leigh wasn't so lucky.

The man seized her ankle as she passed, sending her sprawling, her fingertips scrabbling at the bottom stair. She kicked at him furiously. Owen grasped her wrists and tugged, dragging her after him. Then Leigh's boot struck the man's face, breaking his hold.

They continued their upward scramble.

At the landing, Owen looked back. Both men were thundering up the stairs. Pushing Leigh towards the second flight, he barked, "Keep going!"

There was a vase of flowers on a small table beside him. He snatched it and hurled it down at the pursuers. Sailing over their heads, it smashed on the entrance hall floor. Then he picked up the table and lobbed it at them with all his might. It did a complete flip in the air before hitting the leading man's raised arms and shattering.

They kept coming.

Owen dashed for the next staircase and found Leigh waiting for him at the top.

"In here!" she panted, and shoved him into the spare room. The head of the first man poked above the banister as they slammed the door. Owen turned the key, and they cowered in silence as heavy footsteps approached. There were several sharp raps on the door, then a series of dull thuds as the men began battering it.

"What do we do now?" Leigh asked.

"There's always the window."

"I don't think so. Take a look." Leigh pressed herself to the shuddering door. The rhythmic pounding was relentless.

Owen raced to the window and unlocked it. He lifted the lower half and bent to look out. It was dark, but he could see the flat roof of the shop next door. A straight drop of at least thirty feet.

"Is there a drainpipe?"

"No. And jumping's a good way of getting us killed."

"So's staying here."

The beating on the door grew louder, and now it was mixed with an ominous cracking.

"Whatever we're going to do," Leigh said, "let's do it *fast!*"

"It's flight or fight. And if we can't run . . ." Leaving the window open, he made his way to the wall with the air vent. He knelt and picked up the package he'd discarded earlier. Tearing away the cloth, he brandished the revolver.

"Owen, *no.*"

"With luck we won't have to use it." He emptied the box of shells on the floor. "Stand by the window so they'll see you when they come in."

"Why?"

"To make them think I've got out and you were about to follow me."

"What good will that do?"

"I'm going to be here, behind the door, with the gun. I'll keep 'em covered while you call the police."

"OK." She looked doubtful but did it. The racket from outside grew deafening. The door started to bulge.

Leigh clutched the window-sill with a white-knuckled fist. Owen, who had never handled a real gun before, tried to work out how to load it. After a moment's fumbling he came across a lever that released the revolving chamber. He began sliding bullets into its six empty slots. It was a fiddly job for nervous hands and he dropped two of them.

As he flicked the loaded chamber back in place the door exploded open with a tremendous crash.

It didn't happen the way Owen planned.

Instead of swinging to the right, so he could hide behind it, the door parted from its hinges and plunged forward like a drawbridge. Its top end landed on a pile of boxes, creating a slope, which prevented the two men entering at the same time. But the foremost attacker moved too quickly for Owen to react.

He jumped in, arms flailing, and caught Owen a sharp whack on the jaw. The gun flew out of his hand and clattered to the floor. He turned and made for it. But before he got more than a foot or two the man was on him.

Encircled by a crushing bear hug, Owen saw the other intruder clambering over the fallen door towards Leigh. She ducked out of sight behind a pile of junk.

Fighting for breath, Owen managed to lodge the heel of his palm under his attacker's chin and pushed up as hard as he could. It made no difference. The black-swathed head was like granite. The room spun before Owen's eyes. He could feel the veins in his temple throbbing. He was going to pass out.

"*Stop!*"

Blinking through a red haze, Owen brought the world back into focus.

Leigh had the gun. She held it in both hands at arm's length. And it was pointed squarely at the second man's chest. Owen could see she was trembling.

"Don't make me shoot you," she said. "Just stand back." She glared at the man with Owen. "And you, let my friend go."

Nobody moved.

"I *mean* it." Leigh braced herself.

When the man in front of her took a step forward, it seemed to Owen as though he moved through setting concrete.

Leigh began squeezing the trigger.

The man's arm gradually rose towards the gun.

The weighty revolver was cumbersome, its long-unused mechanism sluggish. Her neck tendons stood out like twine as she applied more pressure.

His outstretched fingers were reaching for the muzzle.

The gun's percussion hammer slewed back a fraction. Leigh's mouth slowly twisted into a grimace of concentrated effort.

The hammer moved once more, bringing it within a hair's breadth of the firing position.

He loomed over her now.

A small, drawn-out *click* marked the hammer's arrival at the point of no return. Then, released, it leisurely arced forward again to strike the base of the exposed bullet.

The gun went off.

The shot was terrifically loud. So loud it was almost beyond hearing, a physical blow that set Owen's ears ringing, and wrenched him back to real time.

Several things happened at once.

The revolver's massive kick whiplashed through Leigh and flung her arms upwards. The man she fired at was thrown across the room and smashed into a heap of cardboard boxes. And Owen's captor tossed him aside like a piece of litter.

His assailant now turned his attention to Leigh. But she stood beyond a mound of junk, the only other path blocked by his fallen companion. The man began sweeping the barrier out of his way.

Owen, winded and on his knees, narrowly avoided

being hit by several bundles of magazines and an old radio. A portable typewriter cartwheeled over and disintegrated against the skirting board next to him.

Shakily, he got to his feet. The man didn't seem to notice. Or didn't care. There was no let up in his frantic efforts to reach Leigh, who appeared in a state of shock and merely stared at him. The gun pointed at the floor and looked about to slip from her limp fingers.

The man who had been shot lay still, his tangled limbs at crazy angles. Owen was sure he must be dead. He tried to push the thought from his mind. All he knew was that they had to get out of the room.

Frenziedly casting round for some sort of weapon, he grabbed the wrecked typewriter's heavy plastic cover. It wasn't much, but it would have to do. Holding it two-handed, he swung it with all his force.

The man still had his back to him, and the cover struck the right side of his face with a sickening thud. He lurched to the left but didn't go down. Owen kept bludgeoning him until his legs buckled and he pitched to one side.

Owen didn't kid himself he'd done more than buy a few precious seconds. He tossed away the cover.

"*Come on*, Leigh!" he urged, stretching a hand towards her. She grasped it and clambered over what was left of the wall of junk.

The felled raider was already getting up. As Leigh smacked to the floor beside Owen he came after them. They weaved around the propped door and on to the landing. Their pursuer's larger build slowed him, and he nearly lost his footing as he squeezed awkwardly through the gap.

Owen saw that Leigh still had the revolver. He took it from her.

The intruder was free of the door now. Owen lifted the gun and aimed high, planning to fire a warning shot. Leigh clamped her hands over her ears. The man tensed, ready to spring.

Owen pulled the trigger.

Another deafening blast. And a jarring recoil that knocked Owen backwards. The man threw himself aside, disappearing from sight.

The speeding bullet zipped across the room and smashed into the window, shattering its upper pane. Leigh and Owen started for the stairs.

And froze after two paces.

What stopped them was a movement on the far side of the room. Something round and dark rose stiffly from behind the debris of boxes.

It was the head of the first man. The man Leigh had shot at point blank range.

The dead man.

His eyes were closed, their fleshy lids standing out like white orbs against the black balaclava. The neck, shoulders and chest heaved into view. Gloved hands tore blindly at the cartons before him.

Then a spasm ripped through the figure and his eyes sprang open.

The spell that kept Owen and Leigh rooted to the spot was broken. They fled. Two sets of heavy footfalls sounded behind them.

Driven by fear, Leigh and Owen bounded downwards, giving no thought to the danger of falling. On the last flight of stairs Owen *did* fall and tumbled to the hallway. He was on his feet again before Leigh reached him. The gun was lost, but he forgot about it. It was obviously useless.

They raced through the open front door and into the street. A vehicle was parked about ten yards to their right. It looked very like the jeep they saw at Springfield Mire. And the driver was dressed in black.

Its headlights flashed on, dazzling them, and the engine rumbled. They sprinted in the opposite direction. Owen glanced over his shoulder. The jeep had drawn up at Leigh's door. Two dark forms hurtled across the pavement and leapt in. Neither showed any sign of injury. The jeep revved its engine and accelerated.

"Can't outrun it!" Owen panted. "Have to get off the street!"

Leigh shouted, "Over there!" and ran towards a neighbouring house.

As they tore along the path, the jeep skidded to a halt, its doors flying open. At the top of the path Leigh turned sharp right, then left, into a narrow alley leading to the back garden. Several dustbins stood against the wall. She vaulted on to them and began climbing over. Owen could hear the men crunching along the alley's gravel covering. He scaled the wall, kicked away the bins, and dropped to the other side.

Leigh crouched below, waiting for him. They were in a dimly-lit lane with a row of garages facing them.

"Quick!" she said, scurrying off.

She led him to a wooden door beside the end garage and wrenched it open. Another alley took them into someone's front garden. It was two blocks from Leigh's house.

Owen had his hand on the gate when they heard the soft hum of an engine. There was just enough time to huddle behind the hedge separating garden from pavement. Holding their breath, they squinted through the leaves.

A car cruised along the road at walking speed. There was no doubt its occupants were searching for someone.

But it wasn't the jeep. It was Ross Waverley's sleek black limousine.

Leigh and Owen stayed hidden until after it had gone. Then they moved off, hugging the shadows, and lost themselves in the silent streets.

13

It was shortly before dawn when they arrived at Owen's house. They couldn't think where else to go. Not that they were thinking completely straight anyway. The last few hours had left them jumpy and confused.

Owen couldn't trust his father any more, so there was the problem of whether he might be in. He solved it by first leaning on the doorbell for a couple of minutes. Then he checked the house while Leigh waited in the hall. They were alone.

But even in Owen's room they didn't feel safe. He noted the paleness of Leigh's face. He supposed he looked just as pallid himself. And just as tired.

"We have to call the police," he said wearily.

"Yes." She rubbed her eyes. "But what if they don't believe us again?"

"They'll have to this time."

"Will they? There's no proof. All we can show them is the damage to my place. They'd only have our word we were attacked."

He sighed. "You're right. But we still have to tell them."

"Why were those men after us, Owen?"

He shrugged.

"And what if they come here?" she added nervously.

"Don't worry about that." He hoped he sounded surer than he felt. "The front door's locked and so's this one."

"As if locks would stop them when bullets don't."

Before he could answer, she said, "And that's something *else* the police will never believe. I don't know I believe it myself."

Owen sat down on the floor, facing her chair. He took her hand. "Look, let's try being logical. Maybe the bullets were blanks."

"Blanks that shatter windows?"

"Well, perhaps the *first* bullet was a blank and —"

"No. They weren't blanks."

"The men could have been wearing bullet-proof vests."

"It didn't look like it to me. Let's not kid ourselves, Owen. There's no rational explanation."

"That doesn't mean there's no explanation at all!" He realized he was getting irritated and paused to calm himself. "Sorry." He squeezed her hand. "Look at it another way. Suppose all the unusual stuff happening in Leyswood's connected."

"How?"

"I don't know. But think about it." He began ticking off items on his fingers. "First, the area gets bombarded by mystery objects nobody can find a trace of. Second, communications start going wrong."

"Professor Saul made that point."

"Right. Then people turn seriously wacko. Like your aunt and uncle, and my dad."

"I can't see how *that* ties in."

"Neither can I, but it's a fact. Now we get these MIBs running around."

"MIBs? Try talking English."

"Sorry. Bit of shorthand. It's just that the weirdos we've come across all dress the same way. They go for black. MIB stands for men in —"

"Yeah, yeah, I get it. So they're making a fashion statement. What about it?"

"It links them. Those guys we saw over the road at Mr Turner's were dressed in black. Not to mention that character Eric and I ran into near Springfield Mire."

"And the jeep that nearly hit us afterwards —"

"Was driven by somebody dressed in black, yes.

And I'm sure it was the same one that chased us tonight. Another thing: don't forget Ross Waverley's limo. He's *got* to be involved in some way."

"Yes, but involved in *what*? This could be a series of coincidences. And what possible connection can there be between lights in the sky and these men in black?"

"OK. Forget the lights. Couldn't the MIBs be a gang of terrorists or something?"

"Who don't stay down when they're shot? Get real, Owen."

He sighed. "No, none of it makes much sense, does it?"

It was beginning to get light outside. "We can't put it off any longer," Leigh said. "Are you going to call the police or shall I?"

He got up and stretched. "I'll do it. And if the phone's not working, we'll go there."

It was working.

Owen didn't even try explaining what had happened. He just told the operator he wanted to report a forced entry and assault, and gave the address. She said a car was on its way.

Back in his room, Leigh was curled up in the chair, looking shattered. "Sorry I was snappy with you," she said. "But I can't get that scene out of my head. I keep seeing that man I shot. And when he got up again ... those *eyes*..."

"It frightened me too, Leigh. But it's over now, and the police are coming. They'll sort it all out."

"I wish *I* had that much faith in them," she responded gloomily.

So did he.

Moving to the tape shelf, Owen said, "Let's play something while we wait."

Leigh had to laugh. "Music! At a time like this. You think it's a cure for everything, don't you?"

"It's good for taking your mind off things. Here, you choose."

She trudged over and ran her fingers along the row of plastic boxes. Pulling one out at random, she fed it into the player. Nothing came out of the speakers.

"You must have put on a blank."

"Oh." She looked at the box. "It's got a label. It says 'ULF'."

"There *is* something on that one, but you won't be able to hear it."

"That makes a lot of sense."

"It's quite interesting really. ULF means Ultra-Low Frequency. I kind of blundered into it when I was mucking about with the synthesizer. There's a tone on that tape but it's beyond human hearing."

"Like those dog whistles people can't hear?"

"No. That's ultra-high, similar to bat radar. This is at the other end of the scale. It's *below* human hearing."

"What's it for?"

"Well, the navy tried using ULF to send messages to nuclear submarines. They thought it might travel through water better than higher frequencies. And I read that, years ago, the CIA carried out some secret experiments with it."

"What kind of experiments?"

"Rather gruesome ones, actually. They found that very low tones could kill animals; white rats, rabbits and so on. The vibration scrambled their insides."

"That's *horrible.*"

"Yeah. But the military couldn't figure out how to use it as a weapon and gave up."

"Thank goodness for that." She eyed the stereo suspiciously. "Is it safe?"

He smiled. "Yes. As I said, they used *very* low frequencies. This is safe."

"Just a minute," she said. "How do you know there's anything on the tape if you can't hear it?"

"It registers on the monitors. There." He pointed to a pair of dials on the amplifier. The needles quivered near the limit of their range.

Leigh was about to ask another question when the doorbell rang. It startled them.

"That was quick," Owen said.

"Be careful! Make sure it *is* the police."

"You bet." He headed for the stairs.

The front door had a security peephole. Owen slipped its brass cover aside and peered through. He saw two silver-buttoned police uniforms. When he opened the door he found one of them belonged to PC Andrews. He didn't know the other officer.

They were stony-faced. And didn't wait to be invited in.

Andrews pushed past Owen. His companion followed, closing the door behind him.

The next thing he knew, Owen was pinned against the wall, Andrews' face inches from his own. The constable regarded him with hard, unwavering eyes. "Where's your girlfriend?" It was a demand, not a question.

"I think there's been some mistake," Owen began, "we —"

"Where *is* she?"

"Look, *we* called you. Why the heavy treatment?"

"*Answer me!*"

Owen tried to move to one side. The policeman grasped his shoulders, spun him around and twisted his arm behind his back. Owen flinched in pain. "You're coming with us," Andrews growled. "Both of you."

The other man, having searched the ground-floor rooms, started climbing the stairs. Andrews tightened his grip and marched Owen up too. Leigh was on the landing. "What's wrong, Owen?" she said, growing alarmed.

"Get away, Leigh! They're —"

"*Shut up!*" Andrews snarled. He gave Owen's arm another painful wrench.

The other policeman approached Leigh and spoke for the first time.

"Don't give us any trouble."

He yanked a pair of handcuffs from his pocket. She backed through the bedroom door. The policeman followed her. Andrews shoved Owen after them.

When they entered the room Leigh had the chair between her and the constable. He flipped it aside, one-handed, sending it thumping against Owen's bed. Leigh retreated, and the small of her back bumped into the desk. She couldn't go any further.

A thin beam of light from the rising sun lanced through the window. It caught the handcuffs the policeman was carrying and for a split second they gleamed brilliantly.

He advanced.

Then stopped, mid-stride. The cuffs clattered to the floor. His hands flew to his stomach and he doubled over, as though hit by a tremendous, invisible blow. A great wheezing outrush of air escaped his gaping mouth. He tottered a step or two before his legs gave way. Fighting for breath, he pitched to his knees, shaking uncontrollably.

Leigh, eyes wide, watched in awful fascination.

Owen, just as horrified, felt Andrews' grip weaken. A gurgling, rasping sound came from behind, and Owen's arm was free. He leapt forwards and turned.

Andrews leaned against the wall next to the door. His face was contorted in agony. Gradually, he slid down, quaking and twitching. Specks of white foam oozed from the corners of his mouth.

The policeman who had gone for Leigh was full-length on the floor by this time. His body, too, was wracked by some kind of seizure, unruly arms and legs thrashing.

She circled him gingerly and ran to Owen's outstretched arms. "My God! what is it? What's *happening* to them?"

He shook his head. "I don't know! And we're not staying to find out!"

But as they stepped over Andrews' quivering form, they heard the front door slamming below. Someone pounded up the stairs.

"Oh, *no*," Owen groaned, "more of them."

The footsteps hammered their way to the landing. A figure appeared.

It was Owen's father. He wore an expression of manic fury.

"*Dad – ?*"

Stewart Carter roared and lunged at them.

They scattered to either side of the door, Leigh tripping over Andrews' outstretched legs. Owen's father threw himself into the room and struck out at his son. Ducking and weaving, Owen managed to avoid him, and got himself to Leigh. She grabbed his hand and scrambled to her feet.

A sound somewhere between a scream and a moan tore the air.

Teeth bared hideously, Owen's father was staggering around the centre of the room. He pressed his hands to the sides of his head, sagged and fell. Tremors rocked him as he lay helpless on the floor.

Owen took a step towards him.

But Leigh said, "No," very quietly, and he knew she was right. Whatever his father had become, he couldn't help him now.

"Let's go," she whispered, "before anything else happens."

As they were about to leave, Owen noticed the red power light of his sound system. The forgotten tape was still turning in the cassette deck. On an impulse, he went over to it.

"What are you *doing*?" Leigh's voice was sharp with urgency.

He wasn't sure himself. But a vague idea was forming in his mind, and something told him the tape was important. He took it out and dropped it into his pocket.

"*Come on!*" Leigh pleaded.

The three men had stopped moving now. Owen took one last look at his father before following her out of the room.

An empty police car stood outside. Its radio hissed and chattered to itself. Apart from that, the street was empty.

Owen said, "Where are we going?"

"Anywhere. Just away from here."

"Right or left?"

"Does it make any difference?"

They turned left.

A bloody red sun was rising above the houses opposite.

They didn't know where to go or who to trust. And they needed somewhere to hide before the streets began to fill.

After wandering for about an hour they found themselves in Leyswood's northern suburb. A newly built housing estate spread out before them. One of its smaller blocks of flats didn't have anyone living in it yet, and there was no front door fitted. Leigh and Owen settled on the steps at the bottom of the stair-well.

"Oh, wow," Leigh said, "it's like a dream. What am I *saying*? It's a nightmare! What the heck happened back at your place, Owen?"

"I don't know. It looked like they were having

some kind of fit." His face darkened with concern. "Suppose my dad and those policemen are . . ."

"Dead?" She gave him a reassuring hug. "I don't think so, somehow. We thought that MIB was dead too, didn't we? I reckon something just knocked the stuffing out of 'em."

"I'll ring later and see if Dad answers."

"Good idea. And I'll try to get Eric. I want him out of there."

"We'll make it a priority. But we've got to get help."

"Who from?"

"Not the police, obviously."

"It's scary when you can't rely on anyone in authority, isn't it?" She snapped her fingers. "Authority! *Of course!* We're not thinking straight, Owen. We'll go to Ralph Saul."

"Yeah! People will listen to him; he works for the Government."

"As long as he doesn't think we're nuts."

"He won't."

"But it'd be best if we stayed out of sight as much as possible," she said. "The police are probably looking for us."

"Right." He glanced at his watch. "It's too early to call anybody now. We'll give it a couple of hours before we look for a phone."

"And hope it's working."

"That *would* be useful."

It was growing warmer. Leigh shrugged off her coat. "Owen, why did you take that tape?"

"I'm not sure. I thought it might have had something to do with Dad and those cops getting sick."

"But you said it was harmless. And they're not laboratory animals, are they?"

"No, but ... this is just a theory, right? Suppose there's some sort of virus going round that made the tape harmful to them. Something that lowers their resistance to the tone."

"That's a bit far-fetched..."

"I was thinking about conditions like migraines, where sound makes the pain worse."

"I don't buy it, Owen. You're talking about a bug that turns people into homicidal maniacs."

"As I said, it's only a theory. And don't forget that Sherlock Holmes stuff Professor Saul was going on about. Once you've eliminated the probable —"

"The improbable must be the truth, yeah. This is a little *too* improbable, amigo."

"Maybe." Owen covered a yawn with the back of his hand. "Look, there's nothing we can do at the moment. Let's get some rest."

"The way I feel right now I'll never shut my eyes again."

"Try."

They rolled up their jackets for pillows and made themselves as comfortable as they could in each other's arms. Despite their fears, they slipped into the deep, dreamless sleep of exhaustion.

It was nine o'clock before they found a telephone box. Although it was early, warm air shimmered above the heated pavements. No clouds marred the perfectly blue sky. The day was going to be hot.

Owen still had the number of Saul's hotel on a scrap of paper in his pocket. And the phone line was scratchy but clear enough to use. As the receptionist put them through, Leigh huddled close and listened. The hellos barely over, Saul said, "I'm very glad you rang, Owen. In fact, I've been trying to reach you —"

"Sorry, Professor," Owen cut in, "this is a pay-phone and I've got to be quick. We have to see you. Urgently."

"And I need to see *you*." He sounded excited. "Do you remember me saying I was forming some ideas about what's happening here in Leyswood? Well, I think the last clue's fallen into place! If I'm right it's ... *incredible*. Almost unbelievable!"

A wave of static rippled the line. "Speak up!" Owen shouted.

"This is important," Saul continued. "*Very* important. I need allies to help me get certain information to the authorities in London. But I don't want to talk about this on an open line. Can you come to see me?"

More crackling interference swept in. "Yes! Where and when?"

"My hotel at midday. Have you got that? Be here at twelve o'clock."

"Yes, Professor Saul! At twelve!"

"But be careful! There may be danger..." His voice began to break up. "... keep a low profile ... Don't —"

The line went dead.

"What do you make of *that*?" Leigh said.

"Maybe he's solved the mystery. But I want to know what he was warning us about. Let's call again."

They tapped out the number twice more, but couldn't get it to ring. "It'll have to wait until we see him," Owen said. He passed the receiver to Leigh. "Why don't you try Eric?"

While she punched the digits, he walked to the edge of the pavement and looked up and down the street. Nobody was around. Then he heard her say, "Hello? Eric?" He turned, and she gave him the thumbs-up sign. Owen stayed where he was, keeping an eye on the road, and caught only her end of the conversation.

"Listen to me, Eric," she said. "Are you alone? Good. And are you all right?" She paused briefly while he answered. "OK," she interrupted, "that's fine. I can't hang about, so pay attention. I want you to meet Owen and me outside the place where Ralph

Saul's staying, at midday. You know where that is, don't you?''

A man puttered by on a moped, but didn't look their way.

"You mustn't tell Aunt Alice or Uncle George," Leigh continued. "Don't tell *anybody*. Understand? There's something else you can do for me. If you go to the bottom drawer of my dressing table you'll find a purse . . . what do you mean, you *know*?'' She sighed. "Look, just bring it, yeah? And be careful. Make sure you're not followed. No, I can't explain now. See you later.''

"Well?'' Owen asked.

"He's OK. Our aunt and uncle are out, so hopefully he can avoid them.''

"What was that about a purse?''

"I thought we could use some money, and I had a few pounds stashed. *If* Eric's left any. It was dumb to think I could hide it from him.''

"You watch the road,'' he said. "I'll call home.'' The number rang for more than a minute, but no one answered.

"Don't worry about it,'' Leigh told him, planting a kiss on his cheek. "You can try again later.''

She scanned the street. A few people were about, mostly workmen. "I think we should get out of here.''

"Yeah, but give me a sec. I've got an idea.'' He called the operator. When she answered, he said,

"Can you give me the number of the police station in Thornbridge, please? OK, I'll hold."

Owen covered the mouthpiece with his hand. "We might have better luck with out of town cops," he explained.

The operator came back on. "Yes?" Owen said, then fell silent for a couple of seconds. "Oh, I see. What about Denton or — Hello? *Hello?*" He gave up and replaced the phone.

"Interference?"

"I think she cut me off. And she said she couldn't connect me with Thornbridge because there's a problem with the long-distance lines."

"Why do I find that hard to believe?"

"Well, it's all down to Ralph Saul now. Come on, we've got a couple of hours to kill."

It seemed like a good idea to lose themselves in the town centre's mid-morning crowd. But it was risky, and they were suspicious of everyone they saw. So they kept moving.

As they walked through one of the turnings off Leyswood High Street, Leigh grabbed Owen's arm and dragged him into a shop doorway.

"What's the matter?"

She pointed over the road. "Look!"

Ross Waverley's sleek limousine was nosing into a parking space. Its brake lights went off and the engine stilled, but nobody got out.

Then Owen spotted a familiar figure swaggering arrogantly along the bustling pavement. "Is that who I think it is?"

"Pete Collins!" Leigh groaned. "Just what we need! Let's get away before he sees us."

"No, wait a minute. Unless I'm very much mistaken..."

Collins made straight for the limo. When he reached it, the driver's window rolled down. The bully stooped and said something to the chauffeur. Then one of the rear doors sprang open and Collins got in. The car edged into the stream of traffic and drove away.

"It seems Mr Waverley keeps some very strange company," Owen said.

15

*T*o the Commanding Officer,

We are writing because the phone lines are down. Criminal events are taking place here in Leyswood. We believe the local police may be involved in some way, along with a businessman called Ross Waverley. Professor Ralph Saul, who works for the Ministry of Defence, will vouch for us and provide more details. He is staying at the Phoenix Hotel.
Our lives may be in danger.
Please send help.
This is not a hoax.

"It looks really stupid when you write it down,"

Owen said. "The cops in Thornbridge are gonna think it's a put-on."

Leigh took the note and signed it. "Not if they get in touch with Professor Saul. They can't ignore a man like that. Anyway, what have we got to lose?" She gave the sheet of paper back to him. "Your turn."

He wrote his name next to hers. "Do we put our addresses on?"

"We ought to."

"But we're not there. And if the police talk to my dad, or your aunt and uncle, they're bound to say everything's all right, aren't they?"

"They're more likely to take the letter seriously if there's addresses. We'll just have to rely on them believing the professor. Do it."

"OK." He printed their addresses along the bottom of the sheet. "All we need now is an envelope and stamp."

"We'll get them on our way to the hotel. What's the time?"

Owen looked at his watch. "Nearly eleven-fifteen."

"We can have ten more minutes then."

She leaned back against the tree they were sitting under and surveyed the park. It was a glorious morning. People sunbathed on the grass. Children played ball games as their parents laid out picnics. A woman swept past on a bicycle, a small dog yelping along behind her.

"Who'd believe anything was wrong on a day like this?" Leigh said. "Everything seems so ... normal."

"Yeah, it makes what happened last night feel kind of unreal. But don't be fooled by appearances. Something bad's going on in this town."

The sun was in her eyes. She shaded them with her hand. "Are you sure about the chauffeur, Owen? You really did recognize him?"

"I'm positive. When that jeep nearly collided with us at Springfield Mire I thought I'd seen the driver before. It's been bugging me ever since. Seeing Waverley's chauffeur this morning, I knew it was the same man."

"That gives us another link between Waverley and whatever's going on down in Leyswood. Or does it? All we know is that one of his employees, and his limo, are mixed up in it. There's nothing to connect him directly."

"That's true," he admitted. "And the same applies to Pete Collins. So we saw him getting into the limo. Big deal. It doesn't prove anything against Waverley himself. Maybe Collins knows the driver."

"That does seem more likely than Collins knowing Waverley. You could hardly find two more different types."

"You can say that again!"

"But even if we haven't got any actual proof, surely everything points to Waverley? He must be in this thing up to his neck."

"I agree. But that brings us back to what 'this thing' is." He checked his watch again. "Let's go. We've got to meet Eric, remember."

They brushed themselves off and walked to the shops. The sub Post Office sold them a stamp and an envelope. Owen didn't know the exact address, so he wrote *Police Headquarters, Thornbridge*, and hoped that was good enough. There was a pillar box on the pavement outside. Leigh checked the collection times. "Good. There's one at half-past eleven."

"Which is just about now." Owen pushed the envelope through the slot.

"Here." Leigh handed him a bar of chocolate. "I bought a couple of these while you were getting the stamp."

Munching the chocolate, they set off for Ralph Saul's hotel.

Had they looked back before reaching the end of the street they would have seen a postal van drawing up at the mailbox. The uniformed driver sat in the cab for a moment, watching them walk away, before he got out. He unlocked the box and began putting its contents into a sack. But he did it slowly, examining each letter. When he got to the one addressed to the Thornbridge police he stared at it long and hard.

A cold smile stretched his taut lips.

As hotels went, the Phoenix was quite small. A modern building, four floors in height, it probably had no more than two dozen rooms. Leigh and Owen walked to the entrance, the searing midday sun beating down on them. They waited until just after twelve, but there was no sign of Eric.

"Let's go in," Owen suggested. "You can leave a message for him at reception."

The woman at the front desk told them they were expected in room 17 on the top floor. A tiny lift carried them up. It was stiflingly hot, and seemed to take ages. Leigh, uncomfortable in the confined space, said, "I'd hate to get stuck in this thing."

She was glad when they stepped out into the heavily-carpeted stillness of the corridor.

Room 17 was in front of them. Owen knocked. There was no reply.

He was about to try again when the door inched open, revealing a figure whose face was hidden by shadow.

"Professor?"

Ralph Saul slowly moved into the light. And they knew.

They couldn't say *how* they knew, but they both felt it. Perhaps it was his face. All trace of kindness had gone from it. The smile was forced, the eyes dead.

It could have been his body. He stood with unnatural stiffness. His arms hung straight and rigid at his sides, fists clenched.

It might have been his silence. He offered them no

greeting, and they could almost believe he had lost the gift of speech.

Whether it was any of these things, or some nameless instinct, was beyond their understanding. They just *knew*.

He had changed.

Saul edged aside and motioned them in with his hand. It was like being beckoned into a spider's web. They should have turned and run. They didn't. They couldn't. The shock rooted them. And maybe in some small part of their minds they didn't want to accept the truth.

As he realized they weren't going to move, Professor Saul's false smile melted away and a look of angry irritation grew in its place. He jerked his hand again, sharper this time. There was no mistaking the gesture. It demanded that they enter.

Leigh found her voice. "We're, er, in a rush, so we won't come in." She shot a terrified glance Owen's way.

He took the hint and thought fast. "Yeah, sorry Professor, but we have to be somewhere in a few minutes. Forgot about another appointment, you know? We just dropped in to ask if we could postpone our meeting."

Saul didn't react for several seconds. Then, with effort, he spoke. "I have ... nothing ... to ... say to you."

"What about your theory?" Leigh said. "You

know, your ideas about what's happening in Leys-wood.''

"All is ... well ... in Leys ... wood.''

Her voice softened. "What's wrong? Are you ill?''
There was no answer. They could see it was hopeless.

"We should go," Owen said.

"*No!*"

The force of Saul's outburst made them jump.
Owen grasped Leigh's sleeve and started to pull her
away.

Saul lurched after them. "You must ... give me ...
something,'' he growled.

"I don't know what you mean," Owen replied.

"*Give me the tape!*"

"How did you —"

"Owen!'' Leigh cried. "Come on!''

Saul threw out an arm to stop them and shrieked,
"*You will stay!*"

They turned and dashed along the corridor. At the
far end, there was a fire door. Owen pushed the metal
bar that opened it and they tumbled through. The
landing on the other side led to a staircase. As they
rushed down the steps, Saul's head poked around the
door above them. But he didn't follow.

Each level had a window overlooking the street. As
they passed the one on the first-floor landing, Leigh
happened to glance out of it. She stopped suddenly,
making Owen swerve to avoid bowling into her.
"What's the matter?'' he panted.

"Look! Down there!" An empty jeep was parked outside the hotel's main entrance to their right. "Do you think it's the same one?" she asked.

"It's too much of a coincidence not to be. Let's move!"

They reached ground level and went out the emergency exit. Grabbing a left, they began sprinting up the street.

"*Leeeighhh! Ooooweeenn!*"

They skidded to a halt and turned. Eric strolled along the pavement towards them. Owen and Leigh dashed to him, took an arm each and frog-marched him away at high speed.

"Hey! What —"

"Don't talk, walk!" Leigh ordered.

The trio got to the top of the road and into the busier streets of the town centre. No one seemed to be following them.

Owen didn't know what they were going to do next. But he was certain of one thing. The Ralph Saul they knew had gone.

And it looked like their last hope had gone with him.

Leigh said, "We've got one or two things to tell you, Eric."

"*That* could be the understatement of the century," Owen remarked wryly.

They had walked aimlessly for a while before deciding to go back to the empty block at the new housing estate. But there were more people about now and it wasn't a good place to hide. Owen kept an eye on the street while Leigh brought her brother up to date. She explained about Stewart Carter's increasing weirdness, and Owen's encounter with his neighbour, Turner. Then she told him about Pete Collins getting into Waverley's limo, and described their run-in with the MIBs and Ralph Saul.

When she finished, he said, "You didn't see the meteors last night then?"

Leigh sighed with exasperation. "No, Eric. We were a bit busy staying alive, you know?"

"Oh, yeah, right."

"Why were you late meeting us, by the way?"

"Well, after you called, Aunt Alice and Uncle George came in. They went on and on about whether I knew where you and Owen were."

"What did you say?"

"I *didn't* know where you were, did I? They really gave me an ear-bashing, though."

"You didn't mention me calling?"

"'*Course* not. That reminds me." He dug into his jacket pocket. "Here's your purse."

She looked inside. "What a surprise." Her voice was heavy with sarcasm. "There seems to be less here than I remember."

Eric reddened. "Ah. Yes. I had to borrow some to —"

"Forget it, I don't want to know." She glumly inspected the purse's meagre contents. "We won't get far on this."

"Where are you going?"

"*We*. You're coming with us. But I don't know where exactly."

"You mean I'm not going back? Cool!"

"This isn't a game, Eric. It's serious."

From the doorway, Owen said, "We better be moving soon. There's too much activity here."

"Do you really think there's a disease going round, Owen?" Eric said.

"Perhaps."

"And Professor Saul's got it?"

"Could be."

"And our aunt and uncle, and your dad?"

"Maybe them too."

"And those MOBs?"

"*MIBs!*" Leigh corrected him.

"Er, yeah, MIBs. But what I don't understand is how catching a bug stops bullets hurting you."

"Neither do I," Owen admitted. "And it may not even be a disease. It's just a theory at the moment."

"But if there *is* a bug," Eric persisted, "what's to stop us getting it?"

Leigh and Owen exchanged uncomfortable glances. "There's no point worrying about that," Leigh said briskly. "The main thing is to work out what we're going to do next."

"Right," Owen agreed. "Unfortunately, I was counting on Professor Saul helping us."

"Why don't we —" Eric began.

"Quiet," Leigh told him. "You know, Owen, I've been wondering how Saul knew about your tape."

"That's been bothering me, too. Not so much him knowing, because the MIBs would have told him, presumably. We saw their jeep at the hotel, remember."

"Couldn't we —" Eric said.

Leigh *sssshhhed* him.

"It's *why* he wanted the tape," Owen continued. "Which makes me think it's important in some way." He tapped the hip pocket of his jeans. "So I'm not letting it out of my sight."

"The question is," Leigh said, "who do we turn to now?"

Eric bobbed up and down in frustration. "I think we should —"

Leigh cut him off. "Put a sock in it." She returned her attention to Owen. "I suppose it's overly optimistic to expect anything from the Thornbridge police?"

"Yeah, we have to assume we're on our own. Unless we can think of somebody else to go to."

"*I CAN!*" Eric bellowed. "Poppy Morgan!"

"Brilliant idea!" Leigh said. "Why didn't you mention it before?"

Eric was speechless.

"And there's no need to shout," she added, "we're not deaf."

"It *is* a good idea, Eric," Owen said. "Maybe we can persuade her to broadcast something."

Leigh grew wary. "But can we trust her?"

"We can't trust anybody. We'll just have to be careful."

"All right, but no phone calls, they're too risky. We'll go there. Do you think we should split up? I mean, three of us might stick out."

"No," Owen decided. "We have to stay together. It's safer."

The journey was a nightmare. There was no way of telling friend from foe. Everyone they saw was a potential enemy. An elderly man, coming out of a house, gave them what might have been an odd look. A shopkeeper glanced their way with perhaps a little too much curiosity. People on the streets seemed to gaze at their faces with more than usual interest. Their home town had become an alien world to them. A world of prying eyes.

"I feel like we're in a goldfish bowl," Leigh complained.

"Just keep moving," Owen said, "and don't do anything to attract attention."

"They can't *all* have the bug, can they, Owen?" Eric asked.

"Maybe none of them have. But we can't tell, so we have to be cautious."

As they walked along the High Street they saw something unusual. A large open truck, painted military green, sped past. Two rows of civilians sat facing each other in the back, with a man wearing khaki watching over them from the tailboard. Owen noticed a snub-nosed machine-gun in the crook of his arm. And he caught a quick glimpse of one of the passengers before the truck disappeared around a corner. "I didn't know the army was in Leyswood," Leigh said.

"Those people looked pretty miserable," Eric remarked.

"Yeah," Owen agreed. "And did either of you recognize any of them?"

Eric shook his head. Leigh said, "No, it was going too fast. Did you?"

"I could have sworn one of them was Mike Adams."

"The guy on the radio?"

"Yeah, I've seen him a few times at 525's studios."

"What would somebody like that be doing riding in an army truck?" she asked.

Owen shrugged. "We'll ask Poppy, she'll probably know. But even if it wasn't Adams, what the heck are the army doing here?"

"File it under mysteries to be solved, along with all the others," she replied. "Now let's concentrate on getting there in one piece, shall we?"

Eric saw him first.

It was a couple of blocks from the radio station and they were about to cross a busy road. As Owen and Leigh stepped off the kerb, Eric grabbed their arms.

"Wait!"

"What *is* it?" Leigh snapped.

He pointed to a shop doorway on the other side of the street.

Pete Collins was lounging in it.

At the exact moment they spotted him, he looked up and saw them. His face twisted into a snarl. He pulled his hands out of his leather jacket's pockets and balled them into fists. Then he began running towards them.

"Why isn't anybody ever pleased to see us?" Leigh said. Collins was on the edge of the pavement opposite, head darting from side to side as he looked for a break in the traffic.

"We don't need this," Owen declared, "not when we're trying to avoid being noticed. Leg it!"

The others didn't wait to be told twice. They turned and ran back the way they'd come. Owen, bringing up the rear, caught sight of Collins weaving through the stream of cars. Drivers pounded their horns. Eric, ahead of the others, reached the first corner and swerved round it. Leigh and Owen followed. Collins pounded along behind.

"At least he seems to be alone," Leigh puffed.

"He's quite enough to handle by himself," Owen said.

They were approaching the High Street. Leigh glanced over her shoulder. Collins was closing the gap.

"Faster!" she shouted, and put on an extra burst of speed.

The traffic in the main road was even heavier. Eric got to it just as a space opened between vehicles, and managed to scoot across. But Owen and Leigh were forced to stop for several precious seconds while the wall of metal flowed past them.

"*Come on!*" Eric yelled from the other side.

Collins was bowling through the crowd on the pavement, knocking aside anyone in his path. A chorus of angry shouts and curses rose in his wake. Leigh and Owen took their chance and dashed into the road. Two cars passed close enough for them to feel the rush of displaced air, but they made it.

A set of lights at the next block turned to red. The traffic reduced to a trickle. They were amber when Collins plunged through the last of the pedestrians and arrived at the kerb. He was less than half-way across the road when they flashed green.

A white delivery van, pushing the speed limit, shot through the intersection. It was no more than thirty feet from Collins before the driver hit his brakes.

There was a tremendous screech.

Collins seemed unaware of what was coming at him. But Leigh, Eric and Owen could see he didn't stand a chance. The van driver spun the steering wheel to avoid a collision.

It was too late.

At the last moment, Collins jerked his head to the left and saw the truck. There was no time to react. The impact threw him a good ten feet before he hit the tarmac.

"He's been *killed*!" Leigh gasped.

Most of the passers-by were rigid with shock, but a few made for Collins' twisted, still body. The van driver, white-faced, got out of his cab and shakily approached it too. Leigh put out a hand and clutched Owen's arm.

A small knot of people gathered around the prone figure. A man knelt, touched Collins' wrist gently and searched for a pulse. The crowd held its breath. The man slowly shook his head.

Owen spoke in a hushed tone. "I know it sounds terrible, but we can't hang around."

"I suppose not," Eric said.

"Collins was a complete nutter," Owen added, "but I wouldn't have wished this on him."

Leigh pushed back a lock of hair that had plastered itself to her forehead. "Yeah. But the way he chased us, the way he looked, it was more than just bullying. It's connected with everything else that's been going on, isn't it?"

"I think so. But let's not get into that now. We —"

A woman screamed. There was some kind of commotion around the corpse. It was difficult to see what was happening. Then the people scattered, revealing what had panicked them.

Pete Collins was getting up.

His limbs didn't seem completely under control at

first and he staggered slightly. But when he was on his feet, he stretched, like an awful parody of someone who had just woken up. There was a hellish expression on his face.

Eric's jaw dropped. "He can't do that. He's *dead*."

A blanket of silence fell upon the onlookers. The van driver hadn't run like the others. He was frozen with astonishment. But now he took a step forward, a helping hand outstretched.

Collins didn't even look at him. He simply back-handed the man aside with a great sweep of his arm. Even for somebody so strong it was a savage blow, and it sent the driver crashing to the ground. As shocking as the action itself was its casualness. It was as though Collins had swatted a troublesome fly.

Ignoring his victim, he scanned the stunned crowd. And found his prey. Owen, Leigh and Eric were mesmerized by the look of intense hatred he projected at them. Then Collins lurched in their direction.

"Oh, God, *no*," Leigh whispered. "Not again."

17

The awestruck spectators fell back to let Collins through.

"I suggest a quick exit," Owen said. "Like, *now*."

"This way!" Eric cried, and ran for a narrow alley separating two office buildings.

Leigh and Owen dashed after him. Collins broke into a sprint, working his burly arms and legs in a powerful rhythm. He didn't look like someone who'd just picked a fight with a two-tonne truck.

The alley fed into a corner of the town square. They went straight across, dodging walkers, litter bins and wooden benches. Collins wasn't as thoughtful. Anyone or anything in his way was shoved or kicked aside. A flock of pigeons took to the air in a confusion of feathers.

Eric led the way to a lane at the far side. Then Owen realized why he was taking this particular route.

The lane's cobbled surface was painful to run over, and should have slowed them, but nobody dropped speed. It sloped downwards into what Eric obviously judged their best chance of escape.

Leywood's bustling street market.

Hundreds of people milled around the colourful stalls. If they could lose themselves among them, they just might get away.

"Stay together!" Owen shouted.

They dived into the crowd. It wasn't hard to tell how far behind Collins was. They could hear outraged cries as he steamrollered into people. And every so often his shaved head reared up above the throng to seek his quarry.

The trio emerged into a less crowded stretch of road.

"Which direction?" Leigh asked.

"Let's keep going along here," Owen replied, "and come out near the park."

"How can he hope to catch all three of us?" she said.

"Maybe there are reinforcements on the way."

"Hadn't thought of that! We've got to get this over with fast."

"Right!"

As they passed a record stall, deafening music

blaring from huge speakers on either side of it, Eric yelled, "Here he comes!"

Collins battered his way through the last of the shoppers. Several people shook their fists at him. He paid no attention. Only those he hunted mattered.

Owen took the lead.

The front of the stalls faced outwards, into the road. He squeezed between two of them and on to the pavement; Eric and Leigh at his heels. Collins came after them.

When he got there, they ran along the pavement and cut back into the road again. For several minutes the chase followed the same pattern. They weaved in and out of stalls at random, from pavement to road, road to pavement, and Collins couldn't tell which side they'd appear.

But he kept coming.

Leigh said, "End of the market coming up. Any ideas?"

"He's bigger than us. Let's go somewhere he can't," Eric suggested.

"Nice one," Owen said. "Look for stalls with a narrow gap between them."

"But we'll have to wait until the last minute before we go through," Leigh reminded them, "to be sure he comes the same way."

They upped their pace. The next nine or ten stalls had no gaps between them. Then they found what they needed: a hot dog stand next to a greengrocer's barrow. The space separating them was about the length of Owen's forearm.

"I'm not sure *we* could manage that," he said. "Not in a hurry, anyway."

"I'll try," Leigh said, and started easing herself through sideways. Owen glanced back. Collins was getting closer. They had only seconds.

"It's tight," Leigh called from the other side, "but just possible."

"You go," Eric told Owen. "I'll come after he sees me."

"I don't think —"

"I'm smaller. I can get through much faster than you."

Collins was nearer. "There's no time to argue," Leigh said. "Let him do it."

Owen had to agree. "OK. But be careful, Eric." He inhaled and shoe-horned himself between the stalls. As he slid out into the road, the hot dog stand rocked a little. The vendor appeared. Short and overweight, his once-white apron smeared with grease, he wore a ridiculously small cardboard cap.

"Watch what you're doing, kid," he warned, a hint of menace in his coarse voice.

"Yeah, all right," Owen said, without taking his eyes off Eric. "Sorry."

The hot dog man was about to say something else but noticed a customer waiting. He stumbled off, grumbling.

The line of stalls prevented Owen and Leigh seeing where Collins was. Leigh, her face etched with worry, called through to Eric. "Don't hang about. As soon as he comes for you, get to us." He nodded.

"Suppose Collins doesn't take the bait, Owen?" she said.

"There isn't another gap between the stalls for at least the next dozen. I think he'll —"

"*Gangway!*" Eric was pushing through, arm outstretched. Collins loomed behind him. Owen grabbed Eric's hand and tugged him free of his pursuer's grasping fingers. The hot dog stand swayed.

Collins wedged himself into the breach. Owen and Eric backed rapidly to where Leigh was standing. Before they could run, the hot dog vendor stomped over, waving a large pair of catering tongs.

"Why can't you walk round like everybody else?" he ranted. He wasn't aware of what was happening behind him.

The trio should have made their escape. But they were held by a kind of hypnotic fascination as the scene unfolded.

Collins was jammed in the gap.

"I know your sort!" the vendor continued. "Getting into trouble and . . ."

Collins had his palms against the side of the hot dog stall. His arm muscles bulged as he pushed at it. The stall shook.

". . . causing me grief! Upsetting the customers . . ."

The stall lifted a couple of inches off the ground at Collins' end. The canvas fringe of its red, white and blue roof flapped.

". . . and making a nuisance of yourselves! I'm sick and tired of —"

A loud cracking sound stopped his flow. Then he realized Owen and the others weren't looking *at* him but *beyond* him. Slowly, he turned.

In time to see Collins upending his stall.

Plastic cutlery, ketchup bottles and stacks of paper napkins hit the road. Collins heaved again, sending a shower of frankfurters and watery fat after them.

The hot dog man seemed to be demonstrating some kind of war dance. He hopped from foot to foot, waving his tongs in the air.

"Damn yobs!"

With a final heave, Collins flipped the stall to his left, crashing it into the road. A metal cover sprang off the back, exposing a blue canister with a rubber tube attached. Two plumes of yellow-white flame spurted from it.

"The gas!" the vendor shouted. He dropped his tongs.

Ignoring the mayhem, Collins strode towards Leigh, Owen and Eric. They backed off, still too mesmerized to make a proper job of running for it.

Beside himself with rage, the hot dog man lunged at Collins. And received a massive fist to the jaw. His cardboard cap sailed upwards. He went down.

Collins stepped over him. A crowd was gathering. At a safe distance.

The greengrocer from the next stall decided to pitch in. As Collins moved away, he leapt on his back, arms around his neck. Collins grabbed the man's wrists, breaking his grip. Next he crouched and hoisted him off his feet. When he straightened again he had the greengrocer over his shoulder. Then he simply threw him at his own stall. It collapsed noisily in an avalanche of fruit and vegetables. Oranges, apples and potatoes bounced off in all directions.

"This is better than the telly!" Eric enthused.

"But imagine what he'd do to *us*," Leigh said.

There was a deafening boom! The ground juddered. An orange fireball went up from the overturned hot dog stall. People shrieked. The stall erupted into flames and billowed black acrid smoke. Small fragments of wreckage rained down.

"There goes the gas canister," Owen said, his ears ringing.

"Let's get out of here!" Leigh pleaded. "He isn't going to give up."

Collins, unconcerned at the chaos, was making for them. But several other stallholders and a handful of passers-by were warily moving in on him. They formed a semi-circle, blocking his path. He ploughed into them. Fists flew. A man reeled back, clutching his nose. Another doubled, tottered a few steps and fell. More people rushed to join the brawl and Collins disappeared under the scrum.

"Let him sort *that* one out," Owen said.

They began running. The wail of an approaching police car sounded above the din of the market.

Leigh sighed in relief. "Thank goodness! They're coming for him."

"Or us," Owen said.

They were careful not to take a direct route in case of being followed, and the rest of their journey to 525's studios was uneventful. But tense.

Before going in, they lingered at the corner of the street to calm themselves, and to make sure the coast was clear. The sun beat down mercilessly. Leigh passed round paper hankies to mop their brows. Owen screwed up his tissue and flicked it into a nearby bin. "It was a smart idea to take us through the market, Eric."

"Yeah," Leigh agreed, "a rare piece of common sense." Eric scowled. "And I've never seen you run so fast before," she added.

"When you're being chased by dead people you tend to!"

"It's pretty obvious Collins has got it," Leigh said. "Whatever 'it' is."

"I don't think there's much question of that," Owen confirmed.

"First we meet somebody bullets can't stop. Now somebody else bounces back, fresh as a daisy, when they should have been totalled by a truck. It makes me more doubtful about your virus theory."

"I've got doubts about it myself, Leigh. But can you think of a better explanation?"

"No. And we're not likely to come up with one out here. Let's go in."

"Just a minute." He flattened back his perspiration-soaked hair. "What exactly are we going to say to Poppy? Without sounding like fruitcakes, that is?"

"I don't know." Her voice was weary. "Only, maybe we shouldn't tell her too much. I mean, she might be OK, but –"

"I know. We can't afford to trust anyone. Do you two mind if I do most of the talking?" They didn't. "Could be we won't even get to see her, of course," Owen informed them, heading for the door.

"Hold your horses," Leigh said. "Suppose Waverley's here?"

"The loud-mouthed jerk?" Eric asked.

Leigh grinned. "That's one way of putting it. But I wouldn't call him that to his face if I were you."

"I hadn't thought of Waverley," Owen said. He

pondered the situation for a moment. "My vote's for going in anyway. Are you with me?"

They were.

Putting down the internal phone, the receptionist said, "Ms Morgan will be with you in a minute." It was more like ten.

When Poppy arrived she seemed a little taken aback. Other than that, she appeared to be her normal self. "Hi, Owen," she said.

"Hi. This is my friend Leigh." The two females nodded curtly to each other. "And her brother, Eric," he added hurriedly. "Can we talk?"

Poppy checked her watch. "Uhm ... OK. But I haven't got much time. And my office's too small for this big a group. We'll try studio two. I think it's free."

When they got there, a look through the glass door confirmed it was empty. They went in and settled themselves among the clutter of broadcasting equipment.

"To tell the truth," Poppy said, "I'm really pushed, and I was going to ask you to make it some other time. But you guys look in a bit of a state. What's wrong?"

"It's a long story," Owen told her. "We won't keep you, though."

"It's not to do with your demo tape is it? Because, as I told you —"

"No, it's nothing to do with that. But it's difficult knowing where to start."

"Try the beginning."

"I'd like to ask you something first."

"Go ahead."

"Do you know why Mike Adams should be riding around in the back of a military truck?"

"*What? When?*"

"Today. They were heading out of town. At least, I think it was him."

"If it was, it's news to me. In fact, he's due in around now. He's doing a show later."

"You've not heard whether the army's in Leyswood?"

"No. And it's the sort of thing we'd be told."

"Perhaps I was mistaken. Anyway, that's not really what we came to talk about."

She leaned back in her chair. "So shoot."

"It might sound a bit . . . ditso."

"You know how it is around here. People are always coming to radio stations with weird stuff. Just spit it out, eh?"

Owen glanced at Leigh. She gave him a nod so faint the others didn't notice. He took it to mean she thought Poppy could be trusted. So did he. Up to a point.

"OK. I don't know if you've come across it yourself, but a lot of people in Leyswood have been acting strangely."

"What do you mean by strangely?"

"Out of character, not their usual selves. Unpleasant. Violent, even."

"And they seem ignorant of basic facts about their families and everyday life?"

"Yes! How did you know?"

Poppy's smile was replaced by a thoughtful frown. "Because we've been getting some rather unusual calls from listeners. When the cursed phone lines are working, that is."

"Unusual in what way?" Leigh asked, curiosity overcoming her feelings of rivalry with Poppy.

"The callers say relatives, friends, or people they work with are behaving oddly. For instance, a woman I spoke to said it was as though her husband wasn't really her husband at all. It was like he was . . . *acting*. She knew it was crazy, but that's how she felt."

"How many of these calls have you had?" Owen wanted to know.

"A couple of dozen, I suppose. But hold on a minute. What did you mean just now about violence?"

"That's where it gets a bit complicated. Our relatives are definitely not acting normally, and I guess you could say my dad's got near to being violent."

Poppy was alarmed. "We're not talking about him abusing you, are we?"

"No, nothing like that. Just incredibly foul-tempered, mostly. We've seen the same thing in other people. Neighbours, one of our teachers –"

"Professor Saul," Leigh added.

"Really?"

"Yeah," Owen continued. "But, as I said, it's kind of complicated, because there are other people around who really are violent."

"What other people?"

"The MIBs!" Eric blurted.

"And who are *they*, exactly?"

Owen felt slightly embarrassed. "It's just a name we've given them. Men in Black, 'cause that's how they dress. They're a gang, and they've been after us."

"A gang of kids, you mean?"

"No, adults."

"Look," Poppy said, "if you're in trouble, the best thing is to go to the police."

"We've tried that," Leigh informed her. "But they're no help. As a matter of fact, we think they're involved with the MIBs."

"Let's be clear about this. You're saying that your families are acting weird. Then there's another bunch of people, these MIBs, who are acting weird *and* violent, and they're in some sort of conspiracy with the police. Right?"

"It looks that way," Owen confirmed. "And it seems to have started about the same time as the meteor business. We –"

Poppy waved him into silence. "You're losing me. Gangs? Meteors? How does all this hang together?"

"We don't know," he admitted gloomily.

"Owen thinks there might be an epidemic," Leigh said. "A bug that turns people funny."

"That's hard to believe," Poppy stated. "I've never heard of a disease that could change its victim's moods in the way you describe."

"That's what *I* said," Leigh agreed.

"Anyway, we would have been notified about it here at the station. The authorities keep the public informed about that sort of thing."

"I said it'd sound daft," Owen reminded her. "But everything we've told you is the truth. Some kind of mystery's going on in Leyswood. We just don't know what it is yet."

"Assuming you're right," Poppy said, "why are you telling me about it?"

"I thought you might be able to broadcast something."

"Such as? A warning about a disease that might not exist? A description of gangs dressed in black? Don't take this the wrong way, Owen, but we couldn't risk panicking people based on what you've told me." She saw their disappointment and her voice softened. "Anyway, it's not down to me. Let me think about it."

"OK." Owen made a decision. "The other thing is to ask a favour." He took the tape out of his pocket and passed it to her. "I wondered if you could make a copy of this for me."

"What is it, music?"

"No. It's something I recorded when I was mucking about with my synthesizer. I won't bore you with the details, but it kind of connects with some of what we've told you. I think it might be important."

"OK. Let's make a copy and keep one each."

He exchanged another glance with Leigh before nodding his assent. Poppy walked over to a high-speed dubbing machine on a bench by the wall. Owen's cassette went into one slot, a blank in the other. The copying process took about half a minute. Poppy flipped out the original, but left the newly-made copy in the machine. "There you go."

He returned it to his pocket. "Er, if it's not pushing my luck, you wouldn't have a portable player I could borrow, would you? You'll get it back."

Smiling, Poppy turned and opened a metal locker. It was filled with an array of electrical appliances, the function of some Owen was only able to guess at. She rummaged through them and brought out a cassette machine the size of a paperback book. It was in a black plastic case with a strap.

"We get tonnes of these things given to us," she explained, "in the hope we'll give the makers a plug on air."

"Thanks, Poppy." Owen inspected it. "It's got a radio."

"Assuming you can get it to work through all the blasted interference there's been lately. Here." She handed him a shrink-wrapped package of batteries. "And now I'm chucking you out."

They got up to leave, Owen swinging the portable over his shoulder.

At the door, Leigh said to Poppy, "What are you doing about those calls you got?"

"There was some talk about a programme item on them. You know, a silly season piece."

"Silly season?" Eric queried.

"That's what the newspapers used to call the summer, when there wasn't much news about. Now it's any quiet period, really. It's when the media starts pumping out stories about the Loch Ness monster, UFOs, skateboarding parrots, that kind of stuff. We would have asked whether the calls were a result of mass hysteria or heat-stroke or something."

Leigh looked offended. "You're not taking them seriously then?"

"To be honest, I wasn't until you lot turned up. Now I'm not so sure. But it makes no difference. Our new boss, Waverley, killed the idea."

Eric and Leigh both started to say something. Owen quickly cut them off with, "Thanks again, Poppy. We won't take up any more of your time." He glared at the others. "Come on, you two."

Leigh took the hint and bundled Eric out.

In reception, Poppy said, "I don't pretend to

understand much of the conversation we've just had. But whatever's going on, be careful, right? And stay in touch.''

She left them in front of the lift. Owen pressed the button. Ten seconds later its door hissed open.

And they found themselves facing Ross Waverley.

They weren't prepared for what Waverley did.

It was completely unexpected. It was repulsive and not a little shocking. It sent shivers down their spines.

He smiled, a phoney mask put on for their benefit. And it reminded Owen of the crafty leer of a hungry wolf.

"Well," Waverley said, "who do we have here? Owen Carter, Leigh Pearce ... and this must be young Eric."

Owen was uncomfortable about him knowing their names. In a strange way he felt it gave him some kind of power over them.

Waverley stepped out of the lift. The trio backed off a couple of paces. Instinct told them to keep their distance. None of them could quite believe the wolf wasn't about to pounce.

"How pleasant to have some of our community's more youthful members visiting us," he continued smoothly. "Particularly when they're so gifted." He turned his penetrating gaze on Owen. "Isn't that so?"

Owen felt patronized, but kept his silence.

"Come now," Waverley coaxed, "no false modesty. I understand your musical talents are quite impressive."

"Er, thank you, Mr Waverley."

"And no doubt you've been working here for a few hours today," the businessman went on. "Or delivering one of your famous tapes, perhaps?"

An alarm bell rang in Owen's mind. "No," he lied, praying the others wouldn't contradict him, "we just dropped in to see ... uhm ..."

"Of course. A social call. I expect you were about to hurry off to your next appointment."

"That's right," Leigh said. "And we're running late, so —"

"In that case, Ms Pearce, allow me to offer you all a lift."

It was a cunning trap, and Leigh had walked straight into it. "We couldn't put you out like that," she replied.

"It's no trouble, I assure you."

"As a matter of fact," Owen said, thinking fast, "we haven't worked out *exactly* where we're going."

"Decide." There was a hint of steel in Waverley's voice. "And be driven there in air-conditioned comfort," he added, in a sweetly reasonable tone. Or what he believed to be one.

"You must be a very busy man. It wouldn't be fair to take you away from your work."

Waverley held out his hands, palms up, in what was supposed to be an appealing gesture. "My duties are light this afternoon. I have all the time in the world."

Owen tried another ploy. "It's such a great day, I think we'll walk. Our parents are always saying we don't take enough exercise."

The lift door started to close. Leigh, who had slowly edged towards it while Owen and Waverley were talking, snatched Eric's wrist. Pulling him along behind, she used her foot to stop it. The door automatically returned to the open position. Eric was bundled inside.

"We shouldn't keep Mr Waverley any longer, Owen," she called.

"Nonsense!" Waverley boomed, a little too heartily. "I see I'm going to have to *insist*." The counterfeit smile began to look strained.

"We appreciate it," Owen told him, "but maybe some other time."

He started for the lift. Waverley caught his sleeve. "If I didn't know better," he said, "I'd think you were trying to avoid me." He gave a hollow, soulless laugh to underline the pretence that it was a joke. "But that would be silly, wouldn't it?"

"Absolutely." Owen tugged his arm free. "I can't imagine anyone wanting to avoid *you*, Mr Waverley." He strode to the lift and got in.

Waverley was right behind him. As Leigh hit the ground floor button he held the door back with his hand. "Are you sure you won't reconsider?" he persisted.

"We're not supposed to accept rides from strange men," Eric announced.

The mock laugh again. "What an original sense of humour." Waverley's smile became more forced. "Surely you're not going to miss the chance of going in a limousine, Eric?" He patted him on the head. Eric gave him a black scowl.

"Careful," Leigh said, "he bites." Eric glared.

Waverley quickly withdrew his hand and let go of the door. Leigh punched the button again and it closed. The lift climbed slowly up the shaft. She leaned back against the mirrored wall and sighed with relief. "I didn't think we were going to get out of there."

"Don't relax too much," Owen said. "There may be some of his buddies waiting for us when we get out."

But there was no one in the lobby. Or anybody looking suspicious on the street outside. They were three blocks away, and moving fast, before any of them spoke.

Leigh summed it up. "That was creepy!"

"Yes," Owen agreed. "Waverley's even *more* obnoxious when he's trying to be nice."

"If we'd been dumb enough to get into his car –"

"Right. And I've got a feeling he wouldn't have been so reasonable if we weren't in a public place. I guess running into us kind of took him by surprise." He paused and added, "I'm sure he knew about the tape, Leigh. That's worrying."

"At least it confirms your hunch that it's important. Trouble is, we can't rely on him not getting hold of Poppy Morgan's copy. Why didn't you mention our suspicions about Waverley to her, by the way?"

"I thought we'd given her quite enough to be going on with. And although she might dislike her boss as much as we do, tying him in with the weirdness could have pushed her too far. As it is, she could well think we're insane."

"She's OK," Eric declared.

"*Is* she?" Leigh said.

"I do wish you'd stop seeing Poppy as some kind of threat!" Owen snapped. "You were prepared to trust her back there."

"Yeah, OK," Leigh muttered. "I suppose I'm a bit paranoid about everybody at the moment." She indicated the portable cassette machine and changed the subject. "What did you want that for?"

"It seemed sensible to have something to play the tape on. I hadn't really figured it out beyond that."

They slowed their pace to catch a breath. And to eye the other people on the streets nervously.

"What are we going to do now?" Leigh said.

"Eat!" Eric demanded. "I'm *starving!*"

Owen laughed. "You should have taken a chunk out of Ross Waverley!"

"He really thought Eric was going to bite him, didn't he?" Leigh grinned. "Mind you, anybody looking at him would think that."

"Shut up, you two," Eric sulked. "Just feed me."

While Leigh and Eric bought food and drinks in a grocery store, Owen tried ringing his father again from a nearby call box. There was no reply.

As they loaded the provisions into their pockets, Leigh repeated her question about what they should do next.

"Unless either of you can come up with a better idea," Owen answered, "I suggest we make for a neighbouring town. Thornbridge, preferably, as it's nearest. Or Denton, if we have to."

Leigh and Eric nodded at each other. "Lead on," Leigh said.

It took longer than it normally would to reach the outskirts of Leyswood because they stayed clear of main roads. Several times they doubled back, or walked in a different direction, in case anyone was following.

They were about to head into open country when Leigh pulled them under the cover of an overhanging tree. A military truck passed, heading the way they'd come from. It could have been the same one they saw earlier.

But this time there were no passengers.

The heat was blistering. Owen took a sip of warm soda and laid back on his folded jacket. Behind him, propped against the trunk of the weeping willow shading them, Eric swatted at a droning bee. The sound of gently running water cast its drowsy spell.

"Don't get too comfortable," Leigh called from the bank of the stream. "We're not staying long." She splashed her feet in the flowing crystal liquid.

Eric tore open a packet of crisps and said, "Why don't we try the radio?"

"Good idea." Owen sat up and reached for the cassette machine. "Expect there'll be the usual interference, though."

At first there was, and he couldn't find a station in

the blizzard of static. Then the set locked on to a clear signal.

"I think it's 525." He increased the volume.

"*. . . with no break in the currently high temperatures and a humidity rating of . . .*"

Leigh padded over and squatted next to them. "That's Mike Adams, isn't it?"

"Sounds like him."

"And this is a live broadcast. So maybe it wasn't him in the back of that truck after all, Owen."

"I could have sworn it was."

"*. . . news and weather again in an hour. Stay tuned for a special item after this message.*"

A naff advertisement for underarm deodorant cut in.

"Funny how 525's the only station coming through," Leigh commented. "You'd think –"

"*. . . important announcement from the Leyswood police, issued this afternoon. The public are asked to look out for three young people who've gone missing. They live locally, and their names are Owen Carter, Leigh Pearce and . . .*"

Eric nearly choked on his crisps.

Owen exclaimed, "What the –"

Leigh shushed him and they listened in a state of shock as their descriptions were given.

"*The police say their continued absence is causing concern,*" Adams went on, "*although foul play is not suspected. They are unlikely to be dangerous, but because of a public health aspect, they shouldn't be approached. Please report any sightings to . . ."*

"Unlikely to be dangerous?" Owen fumed.

"Listen!" Leigh said.

". . . and we have Stewart Carter, the father of one of those missing youngsters, here in the studio."

Owen's jaw dropped.

"Stewart, if Owen's listening to this, what message would you send him?"

"A simple one, Mike. I'd say, come home to your family, son. I know we've had our differences, but we can sort them out."

"What kind of lad is he?"

"He's bright, hard-working and, until recently, well-behaved. But he's fallen in with bad company. So, please, if anybody sees him or. . ."

"Bad company?" Eric said. "What a nerve!"

"Turn if *off*!" Owen demanded. Leigh was nearest. She hit the switch and they sat for a moment in stunned silence.

Then she said, "At least we know your father's still alive."

"That wasn't my dad," Owen responded bitterly. "It just *sounded* like him. He's got to be ill or . . . something."

"Did you catch that bit about public health? Maybe there *is* a plague of some sort."

"Yeah, but we haven't got it. So why make it sound as though we're infectious or something?"

"To stop people getting too close?" Leigh suggested. "And talking to us?"

"If they're worried about that, there must be others like us. You know, people who haven't got the bug or whatever it is, and who suspect something's going on. They don't want us getting together."

"Whoever 'they' are. And that's the point. It doesn't help because we can't tell the difference between them and us. We really are on our own now."

Owen took his jacket and stood up. "All the more reason to get away from here as quickly as possible. Are you ready?"

They were.

"Right then," he said. "Come on, bad company."

Half an hour later they were on the main road crossing Gallows Moor. To their left, Two Stones Hill loomed through a shimmering haze, sunlight glancing off its twin monoliths. Ahead of them, the road began to climb. A little further along it would sweep down again and meet a crossroads. Then it was right for Thornbridge, left for Denton.

"We should go across country," Leigh said. "It's safer."

"That makes sense," Owen agreed. "But have you noticed there's been no traffic?"

"Yeah, where *is* everybody?" Eric chipped in.

Leigh headed off the road. "Who cares? Less people, less chance of being caught. Let's go."

They tramped over moorland, avoiding tangled bracken and clumps of weeds. The level ground soon gave way to an incline and walking became more of an effort.

"We'll be able to see the junction from the top of this ridge, won't we?" Leigh asked.

"Yep," Owen confirmed. "And if we keep a steady pace we'll be in Thornbridge in a couple of hours."

Eric broke away from them and got to the crest of the shrub-covered hill first. Then he glanced down the other side. And instantly dropped to the ground. "What's he doing?" Owen said.

"Mucking about, as usual."

When they got to him, Eric hissed, "*Get down!*" The expression on his face told them he was serious. They flattened themselves. "Look," he said.

There were roadblocks at the junction below. Red and white striped poles had been erected across each of the routes. Police cars and jeeps littered the tarmac. A portable hut stood at the roadside, with two large military trucks parked by it. The checkpoints were manned by policemen and what looked like soldiers. They had guns.

"Wow," Leigh gasped. "And we nearly walked into that."

As they watched, a car came along the road from Denton and stopped at the barrier. Several armed men approached it. The driver leaned out of his window and talked with them. He looked at a sign attached to the roadblock. Then he reversed, made a three-point turn and went back the way he'd come.

"That's why we haven't seen any traffic," Owen said. "They're not letting people into town. Can you read those signs from here, Leigh?"

She shaded her eyes with her hand and tried. "No, they're too far away."

Owen pointed. "Hey, get this! MIBs!" Two men in black were coming out of the hut. They boarded a jeep, gunned the engine and drove into the moor. "They must be patrolling the countryside too," Owen said.

"What about the other road?" Leigh asked.

"It's bound to be blocked as well."

"We could sneak around them," Eric said.

Leigh frowned at him. "Don't be ridiculous."

"I'm the fastest runner. I can get over to the other side and signal to you when it's clear. Then you could –"

"No, we couldn't. Shut up and let us think."

Eric looked grumpy but didn't say anything.

A rumble of traffic came from behind. They turned and saw a small convoy on the road from Leyswood. The television outside broadcast van they'd seen on Two Stones Hill was in front. Two cars brought up the rear. From their lofty viewpoint, the trio were able to follow the progress of the vehicles.

The van and cars were waved to a halt at the roadblock. Firearms raised, the guards surrounded them and pulled open the doors. In a commotion of shouting and argument the seven or eight passengers were forced out.

"I think they're journalists," Owen said. "I recognize a couple of them from the other night. But the police don't seem to be sending them back like that other guy."

Objecting loudly, the reporters were herded towards the trucks at gunpoint. Meanwhile, three khaki-clad men got into the van and cars. They started the engines and bounced off the road in the direction of a nearby thicket. Then they rolled into the trees and disappeared from view.

"They're hiding them," Leigh said.

"Yeah, it's a well-organized operation." Owen looked down at the trucks. "I wonder what they'll do with the passengers."

An angry row was going on at the back of the nearest truck as the journalists were herded aboard. Two guards got in with them, rifles levelled, and brought up the tail-board. The truck moved off, taking the Thornbridge road.

"That's strange," Owen said. "Why take them *away* from Leyswood?"

Leigh didn't respond. She was on her knees, head craning desperately from side to side. "Where's Eric? I can't see him."

"Keep low. He's got to be here somewhere." Owen indicated the low bushes around them. "Probably in that lot."

They crawled through the shrubbery. There was no sign of him. "Where the heck *is* he?" Leigh complained.

Then she glanced down towards the roadblocks. *"Oh, no."*

Eric was scurrying down the hill, bent low and dodging from one clump of brush to another. "The little fool. They'll *see* him. What are we going to do?"

"I'll go after him." Owen started to rise.

"No!" She grasped his coat. "Don't leave me here alone."

They watched helplessly as Eric vanished into thicker undergrowth.

"He'll have to break cover to get to the other side of the road. I don't think he's going to make it, Leigh."

Seconds later, they had a fleeting glimpse of Eric as he emerged some way along the road to their left. He shot over it and through a gap in the hedgerow opposite. No one seemed to notice.

Leigh expelled the breath she'd been holding. "Lucky beggar. I hope he's got the sense to keep going."

She spoke too soon. A soldier crashed out of the hedge, Eric struggling in his arms. The guard shouted something. It attracted the attention of his companions at the roadblock and a group of them ran to help.

"That's torn it," Owen said.

The guards frog-marched Eric to the hut. One of them went in. Almost immediately he came out again. There was someone with him.

It was Ralph Saul.

He spoke to Eric, who stopped wriggling and seemed to listen. Then he drew back his foot and kicked the professor on the shin.

"*Attaboy!*" Leigh whispered. But she couldn't hide the fear in her voice.

Unaffected by the kick, Saul barked an order at the guards and strode into the hut. They dragged Eric in after him and slammed the door.

21

Leigh's face had whitened with shock. "How are we going to get him out of there, Owen?"

He hesitated before answering. "I don't think we can," he said softly. "There are too many of them and —"

"It's my *brother* we're talking about!" she flared. "We have to do something!"

"If we try to rescue him we're going to get caught too, and that won't do anyone any good."

"We can't just leave him."

Owen laid a comforting hand on her shoulder. "Leigh, this isn't a situation we can handle by ourselves. The sensible thing is to get help as quickly as possible and come back for him."

"To hell with the sensible thing!" she snapped.

"And how can we find help if we can't get out of Leyswood?"

"Maybe we *can* get out. There could be another way. Or people back in town we can join with."

"We've been through all that."

"I know. All I'm saying is that if we stick around they'll come for *us*."

"Eric would never tell them where we are. He –"

"They're not dumb. They'll know that if he's here, we're likely to be nearby."

What Owen didn't say was that Eric's captors might force him to talk. He hoped she wouldn't think of that herself.

"If I was in Eric's place," he continued, "I'd want you and him to do the smart thing. And the smart thing is to retreat and regroup."

"He's just a kid..."

"Yeah, but a spunky one. We'll help him best by staying free. We're no use otherwise. Only, we've got to go now, before they start searching for us."

"OK," Leigh agreed reluctantly. She cast a lingering look at the hut's closed door. "Which way?"

"We can't go forward. So let's backtrack and scout off to the side. With luck we might still get to Thornbridge."

They crawled back from the crest of the hill and began their descent. A few minutes later they reached the point where they'd left the Leyswood road.

Making sure the coast was clear, they hurried across it and struck out in the direction of Thornbridge.

The landscape soon grew wild and dense. They came to a thickly wooded area with a rough trackway leading through it. The path was narrow, and dark from overhanging trees. Once they entered, the silence was absolute, and had them speaking in hushed tones.

"What's the plan?" Leigh asked.

"We're walking more or less parallel to the Thornbridge road. But in about another mile it turns away from us. We'll have to come out into the open then and risk meeting more of those armed goons, so –"

There was a crunching sound somewhere in the trees to the left of them. They stopped, senses alert. The sound came again. It was nearer, but they couldn't tell exactly where it was coming from.

Owen passed the portable tape recorder to Leigh. Then he quietly picked up a stout branch. The sound was a constant rustling now. Something was moving towards them. A twig snapped nearby. A little further along the path, bushes rustled.

Leigh clutched Owen's arm.

He raised his makeshift club and tensed. Somebody erupted out of the greenery in a shower of leaves.

"*Eric!*" Leigh cried. She ran from Owen and embraced her brother. "Are you OK? What happened? How did you get away?'' The words tumbled out.

He looked dazed, and didn't speak for a few seconds. Then he said, "I'm all right."

Owen tossed aside the branch. "You're not hurt, are you?''

"No."

"He's had quite an experience, Owen. Tell us what happened in your own time, Eric.''

"I'm all right," he repeated. "They were putting me in one of those trucks. Then a car came along and they were distracted. I ran. I don't think they even knew I'd gone. It was just by luck that I found you."

"Are you *sure* you're OK?" Leigh said again.

"Yeah. But it was scary. And they must be after us. The place is crawling with them.''

"Do you think we could make it to Thornbridge?'' Owen asked.

"I doubt it. I heard them saying they'd got all the roads sealed.''

"What about the open country?''

"That too. There's a lot of them between here and Thornbridge. And Denton.''

"It's back to town then," Owen sighed. "You can fill us in on the way, Eric. But let's keep our voices down, yeah?''

They stayed alert and well away from the road.

After twenty minutes, Owen said, "We seem to have

shaken them off. Either that or they didn't bother following. They know we can't get out of town."

"What did they say to you down there?" Leigh asked her brother.

"Not much, actually. Professor Saul did most of the talking. He wanted to know where I was going, and where you two were. I didn't tell him, of course."

"How did he behave?"

"A bit . . . formal, I suppose you could say."

"Where were they going to take you?"

"I don't know."

"What about the signs on the roadblocks?" Owen said. "Did you get a look at them?"

"Sort of. It was something about public health, like Mike Adams said on the radio. I think I saw the word epidemic."

"That proves you were right about a virus, doesn't it, Owen?" Leigh said.

"Perhaps. It doesn't matter though. We're still on the run with nowhere to go."

Eric said, "I know a good place. And I know how to get in."

Owen and Leigh looked at each other. "We're in your hands," Leigh said.

By the time they got to the outskirts of Leyswood the sun was beginning to set.

22

The nightly carnival in the sky was underway. An endless stream of dazzling scarlet embers cascaded overhead. Leigh was too preoccupied to take much notice. She moved further back into the shadows and scanned the empty street again. Beside her, Owen and Eric scaled the iron gates of Walter Meredith Comprehensive.

"Now you," Owen whispered from behind the bars. After a last look up and down the quiet road, she climbed the metal barrier and followed the others across the darkened playground.

"This is it," Eric said, indicating a grey wooden door.

Owen tried the handle. It was securely locked. "Are you sure we can get in?"

"Yeah, no problem."

"I don't know about this, guys," Leigh said. "I mean, it's breaking and entering, isn't it?"

Eric prised loose a half-brick from the wall next to the door frame. He reached inside the gap and pulled out a bunch of keys. "No. Just entering."

"I can't believe anybody would be so dumb as to leave them in a place like that," Owen said.

"It's the caretaker," Eric explained as he searched for the right key. "He's always losing his set. These are spares. But they only get us into the basement area, not the school itself." He found the right key and opened the door. "And this doesn't lock from the inside."

"That's all right," Owen told him, "as long as it closes. Nobody knows we're here."

They filed into complete darkness.

"What about some lights?" Leigh asked. Eric flicked a switch.

They were in a dingy corridor. At the end of it, stone steps led down to a large, low-ceilinged room. A huge cream-coloured boiler and oil tank occupied one side. Most of the rest was filled with discarded tables, chairs and other junk. There were no windows.

"Well, it's not exactly the Ritz," Leigh decided. "Still, any port in a storm, as they say."

Owen noticed something covered in a tarpaulin

standing against the wall. Curious, he lifted the covering.

"Wow-*wee!*"

Leigh came over. "What is it?"

"Take a look at this!" With a flourish like a stage magician revealing a new trick, he whipped the tarpaulin off his find. A motorcycle.

"Oh." Leigh was far less impressed than she was obviously supposed to be. "It's, er, chunky, isn't it?"

"This is a classic British bike, Leigh," Owen enthused. "A racer, seven hundred and fifty CC, built in the fifties. It's *beautiful!*"

"The colour's unusual."

"Green bodywork and whitewall tyres, yeah. That's the original livery. Somebody's really looked after it, or restored it. Who does it belong to, Eric?"

"Tony Hughes, the caretaker. It's his hobby."

"Perhaps he isn't so dumb after all," Owen said admiringly.

Leigh frowned. "This caretaker. Suppose he comes in to service the boiler, or whatever he does?"

"He's in Spain," Eric informed her.

"You've picked the perfect hideout, haven't you?" she said. "What with this place being closed for the holidays and everything."

Owen returned his attention to the motorbike. "Hey, Eric," he said, "check this out."

Leigh waited five minutes while Owen praised the machine's virtues. Then she said, "If you boys can tear yourselves away from your toy, we need to get organized."

"And to think about what to do tomorrow," Owen added.

"Right. Come on, let's see if we can make this dump a bit more comfortable."

They cleared some floor space and laid their coats out to sleep on. Then they salvaged a couple of battered chairs. What little food and drink they had, along with the tape recorder, was placed on an old school desk. Next, they pooled their money and Leigh counted it. "Three pounds, forty-seven pence," she announced.

"We won't be going on any wild spending sprees, then," Owen observed wryly. "And if this business carries on much longer, how are we going to feed ourselves?"

"Not to mention shelter," Leigh said. "It wouldn't be wise to stay here more than a night. So what *are* we going to do, guys?"

Eric shrugged.

Owen said, "We haven't got many options. First, we can try to stay hidden and hope the situation changes. Maybe somebody coming from outside Leyswood to help, for instance."

Leigh didn't like that. "Doing nothing in other words. And what if nobody comes? I wouldn't rate our chances very highly."

"Me neither. The second possibility is finding other

172

people like ourselves, here in town. We can't be the only ones not affected."

"Trouble is, we've exhausted the list. Who do we dare approach? Mind you," she added as an afterthought, "there's your ... friend, Poppy. Can we rely on her doing anything?"

"Don't count on it. I'm not sure we did a very good job of explaining things to her. And going back to 525's too dangerous after our run-in with Waverley."

"So that just leaves trying to get out of town again?"

"Unless you can think of anything better, Leigh, yes. Tomorrow's Saturday, so there'll be plenty of people around. Crowded streets might be a good cover for us."

"Or it could mean there's more of *them* about. We'd really be taking a chance, Owen."

"Yeah, but what choice do we have? We'll set off early while it's still quiet. And we should consider splitting up after all, to increase the chances of one of us making it. I can't believe they've got every cross-country route out of Leyswood covered. Are we agreed then?"

"Yes," Leigh said.

"Agreed, Eric?"

"I'm with you."

"Good." Owen stood up and pushed his chair aside. "Best thing we can do now is try to rest." He looked at his watch. "It's ten o'clock. Let's get up at six in the morning."

They left one light on, at the rear of the room, and settled down.

Sleep took them.

Owen awoke with a start. For a moment he couldn't remember where he was. Awareness flooded back as he blinked at the basement's dingy ceiling.

A faint sound came from the shadows. Then he caught a fleeting movement at the edge of his vision. His first thought was that it must be Leigh or Eric. Something told him it wasn't.

Whatever it was moved again beyond the circle of weak light thrown out by the single bulb. It was a dark form against an even darker background, but Owen got the impression of a tall, muscular figure. He lay perfectly still. The figure moved stealthily into the light.

It was a man in black.

Heart pounding, Owen rolled from his makeshift bed and leapt to his feet. "LEIGH! ERIC! *MIBs!*"

He bumped into a chair. Lifting it, he swiped at the advancing man with all his might. The chair smashed to pieces against him, leaving Owen holding the backrest. He flung it at the man, missed, and backed off. His opponent appeared unhurt.

Eric and Leigh were scrambling up. Terror swept

the last traces of sleep from Leigh's face as two more men in black lurched from the shadows.

One went for Eric, who dashed towards the farthest, unlit end of the room. The MIB chased after him and they were lost from sight.

The other came at Leigh. She dodged to the side and stumbled in Owen's direction. The ancient desk, covered with their few possessions, stood between them. Leigh frantically grabbed an unopened can of drink and threw it at her pursuer. Although unaimed, it struck him in the face. He didn't stop, but it slowed him down a little.

Owen, busy fending off his attacker, saw this. There were boxes of stationery piled behind him. He began hurling them at the MIB.

Leigh had found ammunition of her own. She pitched handfuls of ancient text books, cartons of ball-point pens and tubs of paper clips. A shower of missiles rained down on the intruders. Bundles of pencils and rulers flew through the air. A large bottle of ink bounced off one of the MIB's arms and shattered wetly on the floor. Sheets of paper fluttered from exploded packages.

Owen and Leigh pelted them with everything and anything they could lay their hands on. They weren't hurting them, just holding them off. And it couldn't last for ever.

Braving the deluge, the men in black charged.

Owen managed to sidestep the one rushing at him.

He toppled a stack of chairs in the man's path and gained a few seconds.

Leigh was hemmed in and had to get around the desk to escape. She wasn't fast enough. Her attacker smashed into her and grabbed her arms. She screamed.

Forced into a corner by his pursuer, Owen yelled, "Hold on Leigh! *Hold on!*"

Kicking and squirming, Leigh fought to break the steely grip that held her. But it was a losing battle. The man began dragging her to the stairs.

Owen's knuckles glanced against the cool metal of an object attached to the wall. He risked turning his head and saw a black fire extinguisher. The MIB almost upon him, Owen wrenched it from its brackets and jabbed it end-first into the man's chest. It was like battering a mountain, and had about as much effect.

"*Owen!*" Leigh shrieked as she was pulled nearer the steps.

He was back in the corner, clutching the fire extinguisher. The menacing figure loomed over him. Then Owen realized that what he was holding could be used as a weapon in more ways than one.

The extinguisher had a plastic pin at its neck. He ripped this out and squeezed together the two levers below it with one hand. With the other, he pointed the horn-shaped nozzle directly at the man's face.

A great *whooshing* gush of snow white foam jetted

out. It smothered the head and chest of the advancing MIB, drenching his black clothing with sticky, milk-coloured liquid. He retreated, temporarily blinded, hands desperately scraping at his eyes. Owen advanced, extinguisher at arm's length, spraying the foam continuously at him.

Sightless, the man lost his footing on the slippery floor and went down.

Leigh screamed again. The third MIB, the one who went after Eric, had reappeared. He, too, had hold of Leigh and they were half-way up the stairs with her. Owen splashed over to them, the spewing extinguisher raised.

It spluttered. Its frothy stream became a trickle.

And stopped altogether.

The man on the floor scooped the last of the foam from his eyes and got to his feet. Spotting Owen, he ran at him. Owen dropped the extinguisher and tried to get out of his way.

He didn't make it. The MIB slammed into him. Owen spun from the impact and crashed against the adjacent wall. A powerful arm came from behind and encircled his neck. A hand pushed into the small of his back. Choking and dazed, it took Owen a second to re-focus. His left cheek was flat against the brick-work. He couldn't turn his head, and the pressure was increasing.

There was a small wooden box with a glass front set further along the wall. He could just make out the red-lettered sign beneath. It said *In case of fire, break glass.* The MIB tightened his grip. Owen found it harder to breathe.

He stretched his arm and swung his fist at the box. It turned out to be on the limit of his reach, but he hit it.

The glass didn't break.

Close to passing out now, Owen knew he had one more chance at best. Summoning a reserve of energy from somewhere, he stretched again, bent his elbow and pummelled the glass.

It shattered.

A nerve-jangling alarm bell went off. In the confined space of the basement it sounded like the knell of doom.

Owen was released. As he slumped, panting, the MIB fled up the now empty stairs. Owen shook himself and stumbled after him.

The school gates were wide open. A jeep was in the playground, and Leigh was being dragged to it by the three MIBs. He turned and ran back to the basement. Eric stood at the bottom of the steps.

"You OK?" Owen shouted over the fire bell's din.

"Yes!"

"They've got Leigh! Come on, we're going to follow them."

"How?"

Owen pointed at the motorcycle. "With this! The key's still in it. But we've got to get it up those stairs.

The caretaker must have a way of... There!" Two planks rested by the wall next to the bike. "Help me," Owen demanded. "Quickly!" They lugged the planks over the stairs to form a ramp.

"We shouldn't be doing this," Eric said.

"What?"

"The bike doesn't belong to us. And we haven't got helmets."

"Give me a *break*, Eric!" Owen snapped. "Does any of that matter, under the circumstances? Now pull yourself together and give me a hand!"

It took all their strength to guide the heavy machine up the planks and into the corridor. As they pushed it towards the door, Eric said, "Just a minute."

"*Now* what? They'll be getting away! And this alarm's going to bring people here any minute!"

"Have you got the tape?"

"Oh." Owen felt for it. "Yeah, it's here. But go and get the recorder for me, will you? And *hurry*!"

Eric did as he was asked while Owen wheeled the bike along the corridor. He came out into the playground as the jeep was driving through the gates and turning left. Eric caught up with him, the tape recorder slung over his shoulder.

"I'll get it going," Owen told him, "then you get on."

He turned the ignition key and stamped down on the kick-starter. The engine sprang to life with a throaty roar. Eric climbed aboard. They lifted their feet and the motorbike moved forward. Owen steered it through the gates and took a left. They could see the speeding jeep's lights several blocks ahead.

"Hold tight!" Owen said, and opened the throttle. They hurtled forward on a surge of raw power. A blast of sultry night air slapped their faces.

Above them, the heavens bled from a hundred crimson gashes.

Poppy yawned and looked at the studio clock. 4.30 a.m. At least another hour before she could go home. Working all afternoon and evening, then doing a night shift, was exhausting. Not that she had much choice. There was always someone to cover for during the holiday season. But she didn't mind. She'd managed to grab a couple of hours sleep earlier, and there really wasn't a lot to do overnight. The station was more or less on automatic, pumping out recorded music. She just had to keep an eye on things until her relief came. In fact, Poppy rather liked being there alone. The quiet gave her a chance to get some paperwork done.

And to think.

What occupied her thoughts at the moment was

Owen and his friends. She didn't know what to make of the conversation she'd had with them. It was bizarre. Yet they seemed sincere. And, unless she was mistaken, frightened. After they'd gone, her ratbag of a boss, Waverley, came in. He'd asked whether Owen had given her a tape. Cross-examined her would be a better description. She'd denied knowing anything about it. Partly because she couldn't stand Waverley and didn't trust him, but mostly because she'd promised Owen to look after it.

Then there was the announcement that Owen and the others were being hunted by the police. She tried to find out more from Mike Adams, but he was tight-lipped. Quite moody, actually. So she didn't mention the business about the military truck. It was all very puzzling.

Now she had a chance to listen to the tape with nobody else around. It might help her understand what was going on.

She took it out of her handbag and fed it into the machine. When no sound came from the speakers she fiddled with the volume, balance, treble, bass and every other control she could think of. All she got out of it was a hiss. Could Owen have given her a blank by mistake? Unlikely. And she was inclined to believe him when he said it was important. Ross Waverley certainly seemed to think so.

Bearing that in mind, she decided to make another copy to keep at home. Just to be on the safe side.

Poppy rewound the tape and switched to high-speed dub. She put a fresh blank into the other slot and jabbed *record*.

"Ms Morgan?"

She spun around, her heart in her mouth.

Ralph Saul was standing behind her.

Struck mute by the fright he'd given her, Poppy just stared at him.

"Pardon me," he said. "Did I startle you?"

Taking a deep breath, she steadied herself. Anger rose in her now. *"Yes, you damn well did!"*

He regarded her with vacant, unsmiling eyes. Poppy realized she was clutching at the edge of the desk, and let go. "How did you get in?" she demanded. "The place is supposed to be locked."

"I can assure you it wasn't." She didn't believe him. The studio was *always* locked at night.

"But don't worry," he continued, "I took the liberty of securing the door behind me."

There was something about his manner that made her uneasy at the thought of being alone with him. She tried not to show it. "What do you want, Professor Saul? It's an odd hour for a visit."

"Well, I've always been a bit of a night bird. And I needed to be sure of seeing you."

She wondered how he knew she'd be there. She hadn't known herself until a few hours ago. "Why me in particular?"

"I'm here on an errand for a mutual friend."

"Really? Who?"

"Owen Carter. He would like his tape returned, having given it to you in error. I offered to pick it up for him."

Poppy didn't buy a word of it and tried stalling him. "His demo tape, you mean? I didn't know you were a music fan."

"No, Ms Morgan." Saul's voice was a little more hard-edged. "I'm referring to another tape I believe you have in your possession."

"This other tape I'm supposed to have, when exactly did Owen ask you to collect it, Professor? Because, as you must know, he and his friends are being sought by the police. If you've seen him recently, have you reported it?"

Had she blinked, the flash of rage that passed over his face would have been missed. He put on an unconvincing smile and said, "I'm afraid you've seen through my clumsy attempt to fool you. But please believe that I did it to spare your feelings. I'll be honest, even if it shatters your faith in Owen. The fact is that the tape in question is mine. He and his friends stole it from me. At my hotel."

Poppy thought how different he seemed compared to the last time they met. She wouldn't have believed him capable of such a foul lie. "I still don't know what you're talking about," she said.

"Let's stop playing games, Ms Morgan. I know Carter and the others were here yesterday and –"

She got up. "I think we're wasting each other's time. And I've got things to do even if you haven't."

He stood his ground. "That tape is extremely important. Hand it over and we'll say no more about it. There'll be no need to involve the authorities."

It was an obvious threat. "The police, you mean?"

"Yes. And your employer, Mr Waverley. If I were to go to him and explain how you've received stolen property, I'm sure your job here would be at an end."

Suddenly she understood how Saul knew she'd be there, and how he'd got into the building. "You go right ahead and talk to my boss, Professor Saul. Do whatever you want. Only I'm going to have to ask you to leave now."

Somehow, she hadn't noticed until then that he had edged nearer to her while they were talking. She felt a chill of apprehension.

"I'm afraid I can't do that," he said.

24

Owen thought he'd lost the jeep. They were trailing it at a safe distance in case the MIBs realized they were being followed. But he had never ridden such a powerful bike before. It needed all his concentration, and he'd allowed too big a gap to build up.

The jeep turned a corner about six blocks ahead. When Owen and Eric got there they found themselves on an apparently empty road. A panicky moment went by without sign of their quarry. Then Owen spotted red brake lights at the junction they were approaching and dropped speed.

It was the jeep, turning another corner. They were in Leyswood's maze of suburban streets now and heading out of town. There wasn't much other traffic around at this hour. But occasionally they passed people standing on the pavements, or in their front gardens, gawping at the colourful sky. Whether any of them noticed two suspiciously young motorcyclists without helmets, Owen couldn't tell. He didn't care. All that mattered was rescuing Leigh.

The houses became less numerous, and they were spaced further apart. Concrete and glass would soon give way to trees and moorland. And it would be easier for the MIBs to notice someone was after them.

When they did finally get out into the countryside, Owen decided to do something he normally wouldn't dream of. He switched off the bike's headlamp. It was incredibly dangerous. But it increased their chances of not being seen. Owen kept well into the left-hand side and hoped nobody was coming the other way. Going round bends was particularly nerve-racking.

Away from the glare of the town, the mysterious aerial objects looked even more impressive. They cut the sky's blackness in every direction, leaving their vaporous trails to fade in the still air. The unmistakable outline of Two Stones Hill came into sight. One or two man-made lights twinkled feebly on its flat summit, no match for the spectacle above. Any watchers were having quite a show laid on for them.

Owen increased speed, knowing that the highway they were on eventually came to the roadblocks.

What would he do then? He decided to keep tracking the jeep until forced to make a decision.

A thickly wooded area began to the left of the road, blocking the view of the hill.

At that moment he became aware of a high-pitched sound somewhere to their right and in front of them. It was a noise he couldn't identify. But it was shrill enough to cut through even the bike's thumping engine. And it was getting louder.

He chanced to look in the direction the sound was coming from. One of the fiery-red oval shapes hung lower in the air than the others. It was hard to say how big it was or how far away. But from this distance it seemed about the size of a ping-pong ball.

Owen checked the road was clear, slowed down, and looked again. The red sphere now resembled a cricket ball. The sound was louder still. They were almost level with it.

Between glances at the road, Owen watched the orb's mass grow until it became a crimson football. The noise, like a whistling rush, was so loud it was all that could be heard.

There was no doubt about it. The thing was coming straight towards them. Even as the thought occurred to him he realized it was too late to take evasive action.

With a brain-jarring screech, the flaming globe shot across the road ahead, slicing downwards at an acute angle. Instinctively, Owen ducked, and imagined Eric must have done the same. The bike swayed, and he had to struggle to maintain control.

The shrieking fireball plunged into the wood on their left. Its dazzling light sliced deep into the jumble of trees, flickered and died.

Owen remembered to breathe again. And tried not to think about what would have happened if they'd been at the spot where the object skimmed over the road a second earlier.

"You OK?" he called back to Eric.

He seemed to be, as far as Owen could tell from his wind-buffeted reply. The incident had put them a little too far behind the speeding jeep again.

Blinking away the lingering glare in his eyes, Owen accelerated.

Anger and fear. Poppy was torn between the two emotions. She was angry at Saul for coming into her place of work with his lies and demands. But feared what he might do if she defied him. He was standing too close to her. It made her feel uncomfortable. Threatened.

"We can avoid all kinds of unpleasantness," he said, "if you simply give me that tape."

She looked over his shoulder at the studio door and weighed up her chances of getting to it.

Saul could see what she was thinking. "I wouldn't advise it, Ms Morgan. You're not going anywhere until I get what I came for." From behind his spectacles, bleak eyes bored into her.

"If you don't get out of here," she said, trying to sound determined, "I'll ring the police."

"Be my guest." He waved a hand at the telephone on the desk beside her.

Poppy wouldn't put it past him to stop her if she tried, but decided to call his bluff. "Right, I will."

She picked up the receiver. It was dead. Rattling the handset only got her a burst of static. She slammed it down and glared at him.

"There is no one to help you," he told her smugly. "And I am but one of many. You cannot fight us."

Was he mad? Or ill in some way, as Owen hinted? Suffering from delusions, perhaps? Poppy tried playing for time to give herself a chance to think. "These other people, who do you mean, exactly? Your defence contacts?"

He hesitated before replying. "Yes. Precisely. Powerful people you would be wise not to upset."

"What do they want the tape *for*?"

"It belongs to them, they have a right to it. And it contains vital ... *data*."

She could see he was lying through his teeth. "Vital, yet you were so careless with it?"

"You are testing my patience!" he barked. "I do not have to explain myself to you!"

"Maybe not," she snapped, "but you could try telling me the truth!"

The telephone rang. It startled her. And she was baffled that it now seemed to be working when just a moment ago it wasn't. She reached for it.

Saul barged in and plucked up the receiver.

"*Hey!*" she exclaimed indignantly. The menacing look on his face stopped her from trying to take it from him.

"Yes?" he said into the mouthpiece. "Ah, yes." He paused. "No. No, she won't." It was obvious he was talking about her. "Yes, that may be best," he agreed with the caller. "I will. Right away."

Then Saul surprised Poppy by offering her the phone. "It's for you," he said.

Puzzled, she took it and said, "Hello?"

"*Morgan?*"

The one word was enough for her to recognize the voice of Ross Waverley. A colony of butterflies began flapping around in her stomach.

"Er, yes, Mr —"

"*Listen to me. I know you lied to me earlier when I asked about the Carter boy's tape. And now I understand you're doing the same with Professor Saul. You will give him the tape or —*"

"But Mr Waverley —" she started to protest.

"*Keep quiet and do as you're told! If not, you'll answer to me! Hand over that tape!*" He hung up.

She stood there with the phone in her hand, thinking of all the witty put-downs and sarcastic remarks she should have made, thinking of how she should have told the repulsive swine what to do with his lousy job. But she hadn't, and she felt stupid and dazed.

"Ms Morgan?"

"Hmmm?"

"Mr Waverley wants me to ring him back as soon as you've given me the tape."

Poppy came out of her trance and slowly replaced the phone.

"And I trust you'll do as your employer tells you," he added smoothly.

"I, er..."

"Why make life hard on yourself?" Saul had adopted a sweet-talking attitude, but it barely concealed the harshness beneath. "Just tell me where it is and I'll take it. That way, you haven't broken any promises you may have made to young Carter. You wouldn't actually be *giving* it to me."

She stared at him, unable to think of a response. "*Well?*" he said.

25

They sped on across Gallows Moor. Strokes of fire were still etching themselves on the dark canvas of the night sky.

In a matter of minutes they'd reach the first roadblock. But Owen had made up his mind to try getting through it. When it came into view he'd pull over and consult Eric. If he didn't want to take the risk, Owen was going on alone. Perhaps, with speed and agility, he could weave the motorcycle through the obstacles. The alternative was going back, abandoning Leigh and almost certainly getting caught. What did he have to lose?

But the jeep slowed and turned off to the right before reaching the roadblock. It took a little-used road, in reality not much more than a dirt track, and bounced into the heart of the moor.

Owen knew what lay at the end of the path, although he hadn't been there for years.

They passed an old, weathered sign reading *To the Abbey*. Monkshood Abbey. Ruined, and abandoned long before he was born. Owen had sometimes played there as a child. He remembered it as a sinister, foreboding place that most local kids would think twice about going to in daylight, let alone at night.

He recalled something else. A house had been built next to the abbey a couple of years ago. Dunnington Hall. As he hardly ever came to this part of the moor these days he'd never seen it. But he thought he knew who lived there. If he was right, one piece of the puzzle might be about to fall into place.

They came to a sharp bend in the track. Rounding it, they caught their first sight of the ancient abbey, towering darkly above a cluster of trees. Owen cut the engine and they climbed off.

"What do we do with the bike?" Eric said.

"We'll wheel it until we find a hiding place."

One on either side of the machine to steady it, they set off.

"Did you know there was a fairly new house along here?" Owen asked.

Eric shook his head.

"Well, there is. It's got to be where they've taken Leigh. And I think I know who it belongs to."

"Who?"

"Let's get ourselves off this track and scout ahead. We can talk then."

In the depths of the trees they pushed the bike from the path and hid it behind some bushes. As they walked away, Owen remembered something and ran back. He removed the ignition key, shoved it inside his left sock and caught up with Eric.

The trees thinned and they could see buildings in the clearing beyond. Using some scrub for cover, they surveyed the scene. A massive stone wall, with two smaller side walls projecting from it, was all that remained of Monkshood Abbey. Four large gaping apertures, once containing stained-glass windows, yawned blankly at them.

To the ruin's left, surrounded by its own wall, stood Dunnington Hall. Anyone hearing the name might picture it as a traditional country manor. They would have been wrong.

The house was ultra-modern and almost shockingly daring in design. A great deal of it appeared to consist of glass, and much of the structure was low-rise. There hardly seemed to be a straight line in it, giving the impression of graceful sweeping curves. Placing Dunnington next to the ruins of such an old building further stressed its modernity. Owen thought it had a strange, futuristic beauty.

"Like something out of a science fiction movie, eh?" he whispered.

"Yeah."

There was a pair of solid-looking black metal gates in the centre of the wall. They were closed. "Doesn't look that easy to get into, does it?" Owen said.

"No."

"We'll have to give it some thought."

"Right."

Owen glanced up at the flaming bombardment overhead and they sat in silence for a moment. "We need to put our heads together and figure out what to do next. My suggestion is that we get round the back and see if there's another –"

The gates began to open. A jeep drove out. It might have been the same one they'd followed, but it looked as though there was just a driver inside. As it moved along the track, the gates closed behind it.

"They're electric," Owen said. He pointed to a small grey box mounted on the wall. "That's part of the operating mechanism."

"Perhaps we can sneak in when they open again," Eric suggested.

"*If* they open again. And it'll be dawn soon. Best to do it before it gets light."

"How?"

"I think I could make the gates work from that box."

"Won't it have a security code or something?"

"The trick is to go round that. From what I know about electronic stuff, I reckon we could get it to short-circuit."

"There could be an alarm on it."

"Yeah, there could. Or the gates could be locked on the inside. Or maybe somebody's standing right behind them. There're all sorts of reasons why we might not make it, Eric, but we should at least try. It's better than doing nothing."

"Won't you need tools?"

"No." He pulled a metal comb out of his pocket. "This'll do. These systems are a lot simpler than most people think."

"What about *that*?" Eric indicated a video camera on top of the wall.

"Yeah, I noticed it. But it's not a swivel one, it's pointed at the road. If we go in from the right, and keep low, we'll be in the blind spot."

"OK. When?"

"Now. You stay here and keep watch. If I can get the gates to open, I'll signal to you to follow. Got that?"

"Yes."

"But if they catch me, run. There's no sense in them getting all of us. What you do then is up to you. Perhaps you could hide in town somewhere. Wish me luck."

Owen scrambled out of the bushes, looked left and right, then quickly dashed for the wall. Bent double, he kept well away from the camera. He reached the grey box and set to work. The comb slipped easily into the casing, and with a little effort its cover came off. Owen studied the circuit board and spaghetti of wires inside.

It took him a few minutes to work out what to do. As far as he could tell, it was a matter of disconnecting a white wire and a green wire, and swapping them. Using the comb's edge as a screwdriver, he started to do it. It was a fiddly job, made harder by the lack of light, but eventually he managed it. All he had to do now was touch the green wire to the white wire's terminal. That would send a command for the gates to open.

He hoped.

Checking that Eric was still where he'd left him, he brushed the exposed end of the wire against the copper terminal. Little blue sparks crackled around it. There was a faint click and a low rumble. The gates began to move inwards. No alarm bells or sirens went off.

Owen edged along the wall and took a peek inside. There didn't seem to be anybody about. He gave Eric the thumbs-up and waved him over.

The gates were fully open by this time. Eric slapped into the wall beside him. "What happens when they find them open?" he panted.

"We can't do anything about that. Come on."

They crept through the entrance. A curving gravel

drive skirted a lawn on its way to the house. They stepped on to the grass verge to avoid crunching footsteps. There were lights on in various parts of the house, but no movement that they could see. Several vehicles were parked outside the front door. Owen recognized one of them immediately. A black stretch limousine with smoked windows.

"I *knew* it!" he whispered. "This is Waverley's place!"

Poppy was on the spot. Saul stood in front of her, arms folded across his chest, and said, "Let's put an end to this farce. Give me the tape."

"You and Ross Waverley are making a big mistake," she bluffed, "'cause I don't know what you're talking about."

Ignoring her, he scanned the studio. "Is it here? Or in your office, perhaps?"

"I can't help you."

He fixed her with an icy stare. "If I have to, I'll bring in people, an army of people if necessary, to search every inch of this place. And your home too, if it comes to that."

"Look," she said, trying to sound reasonable, "why don't we go to the police together and let them sort it out?"

"There isn't time."

"Why?"

"It's a question of ... national security."

She almost laughed at this new twist in his story. "*Gosh*," she said sarcastically, "the stakes are going up all the time, aren't they? Now the fate of the nation hangs on a teenager's tape recording."

"You're meddling in things you don't understand, Ms Morgan!" He practically spat the words. "I *must* have that tape! Now!"

The way he said it gave Poppy a sudden insight. Perhaps he and the people he represented wanted the tape because there was something about it that *threatened* them. Remembering her conversation with Owen, she decided to probe a little.

"Did you know we've had some strange reports from members of the public recently? Maybe you heard about them from your friend, my boss?"

"Don't change the subject!"

"I don't think I am, Professor. And, as a scientist, a seeker of truth, this will probably interest you. These reports are about people in Leyswood behaving oddly."

"I know nothing about that."

"Don't you? There's even a theory that there could be an illness, or something, which changes people's characters. Violently, in some cases."

"*Nonsense!*"

She'd touched a raw nerve. "I wondered if this tape might have something to do with it."

Saul glowered at her.

"Just a thought," she said, leaning back against the

desk and hoping she looked casual. "Anyway, I've given your request consideration and —"

"It's not a request, Ms Morgan, it's a demand!"

"I've considered what you've had to say, and I'm afraid all I'm prepared to do is go to the police with you and put it in their hands. But I can't leave here until my relief arrives. So why don't you come back later?"

Poppy saw the muscles in his shoulders tense. She knew what he was going to do a split second before he did it.

He leapt at her.

And crashed into the empty desk. She'd managed to dodge. Heart pumping, she raced for the door. She had it half open when he caught her. He snatched a handful of her braided hair and tugged it painfully. His arm whipped around her waist and he dragged her across the room. He was incredibly strong, and her struggles were useless. She knew there was no point in screaming. Apart from there being no one else about, the studio was sound-proofed.

He slammed her against the desk. Pain stabbed her back. Then he put his hands to her throat, his frenzied face inches from hers, and squeezed.

Oh, my God, she thought, *he's going to kill me.*

26

Dawn was breaking. The skies were quieter now, disturbed only by the occasional stab of flaming crimson.

Owen and Eric stealthily approached the house. Somehow, they had to get inside. But trying the front door was obviously far too dangerous. They were about to search for another way in when they heard the sound of gravel being crushed underfoot. At least one person was coming round the side of the building.

"*Over there,*" Owen whispered, indicating a row of shrubs next to the drive. They took cover.

Two men in black appeared. Owen knew one of them. It was the man he'd first seen acting as Waverley's chauffeur outside Radio 525's studios.

And, later, driving the jeep near Springfield Mire. Fortunately, the MIBs couldn't see the gates from this angle.

Silent and impassive, the pair walked past the door and on to the other corner. They turned it.

"They're patrolling the place," Owen said. "Let's follow them. They might lead us to another entrance."

Eric nodded agreement.

Owen got to the corner first and gingerly peered round. He found himself looking down a path formed by the house on his left and bushes on the right. Further along, the track met a facing wall and turned at a right-angle through a gap in the hedge. The wall had a set of open French windows. Waverley's chauffeur stepped in. The other MIB stayed on the path and disappeared from sight.

Owen and Eric crept towards the windows, slipping into the bushes just before they reached them. Their hiding place was near enough to the house that they could see clearly inside. What they saw was a luxuriously furnished study. And Ross Waverley.

He was sitting at an imposing antique desk, the MIB chauffeur standing beside him. They were having a conversation, but the words were indistinct. Careful not to attract attention, Owen led Eric nearer to eavesdrop. What they heard didn't make much sense.

"... and use Waverley's radio station more than

we have," the businessman was saying. "And it might be time to get rid of his car. Apparently it's too unusual and –"

Owen was baffled. He put his mouth close to Eric's ear and whispered, "Why's he talking about himself as though he was another person?"

Eric shrugged.

The chauffeur said something they couldn't hear. "Our Saul's taking care of that now," Waverley answered. "And I've sent back-up."

Our Saul? Owen couldn't figure it out. Had they blundered into a lunatic asylum?

Then the name *Pearce* drifted out to them. The rest was unintelligible. Owen was thinking about trying to get closer when Waverley got up and left the room, the other man at his heels.

"This might be our only chance to get in," he told Eric. "Are you with me? Or would you prefer to stay here?"

"No, I'll come."

They scurried to the French windows and cautiously entered.

There were three doors leading from the room. They didn't try the one Waverley had left by. The chances of meeting him were too great. Another was set in a corner, partly hidden by a hanging drape. It was locked. The third, behind the desk, was already slightly open. Owen didn't know whether to be relieved or disappointed on discovering it was a deep cupboard. All it held was a few shelves of stationery and oddments.

"Doesn't leave us much choice, does it?" he said. "We'll have to use the same door he did."

He walked over to it and gently clasped the handle. Then let go again and hastily backed away. There was a murmur of voices outside, and they were coming closer.

He quickly hustled Eric to the cupboard. They'd barely made it before Waverley came back into the room. His chauffeur followed, and there were more people beyond them. Through the crack of the partially opened cupboard door, Owen and Eric watched the scene unfold.

"Bring her in!" Waverley snapped.

Two MIBs dragged a struggling figure through the entrance.

It was Leigh.

Owen tensed. He seriously considered charging in and attempting a rescue. But he knew the odds were overwhelming.

"Get *off* me!" she protested loudly. "Let me go, you ... *dweebs*!"

The MIBs tightened their hold on her flailing arms. Eric opened his mouth, as though to shout something. Owen clamped his hand over it.

"Do be quiet," Waverley told Leigh. "We have much more important things to consider than your feelings." He addressed the guards. "Put her over there."

They marched her to a chair and forced her to sit. Waverley towered over her. "Let me make one thing clear. You are not leaving here. So there's no point in refusing to co-operate with us."

"If you're not going to let me go," she said defiantly, "there's no reason to answer your dumb questions, is there?"

"Oh, but there is," he replied smoothly. "Because I can make things very uncomfortable for you." He flashed a wicked, twisted smile. "Very uncomfortable *indeed*."

"Go suck a doorknob!" she snarled.

"Enough of this! We intend to locate the tape recording your friend Carter made. Where is it? And have any copies been made? If so, who has them?"

"Tape?" she repeated in mock innocence. "What tape?"

"Don't pretend to be stupid, girl! In any event, Carter will give it up soon enough now he knows we have you."

"If you really believed that, you wouldn't be grilling me. He'll *never* hand it over!"

"It will go all the worse for you if he doesn't."

"Threaten me as much as you like, Waverley, you won't get away with this!"

"And what exactly do you intend doing about it?"

"It isn't me, it's the authorities. The police. You

might have them in your pocket here in Leyswood, but —"

"Stop your pathetic whinging. Soon, we will be the only authority."

The telephone on his desk rang. He impatiently motioned one of the MIBs to answer it. The man picked up the receiver, listened, and replaced it without uttering a word. He nodded at Waverley.

"It seems we have another incoming batch to attend to," he announced to the others. In the stifling confinement of the closet, Owen wondered what he could possibly mean.

"No useful purpose is served by wasting time with this one," Waverley continued, casting a contemptuous glance at Leigh. "I shall make her ready."

He pulled open a drawer in the desk and produced a plastic hypodermic gun, the kind used for mass inoculations. Leigh stiffened when she saw it. Then began to struggle afresh. Owen watched in horrified fascination as Waverley placed the instrument against her trembling arm and pulled the trigger. There was a muffled *pop* and a brief hiss.

Whatever it contained, the injection took effect instantly. Leigh's eyes glazed over, her head lolled and she slumped forward.

Waverley put the hypo gun back in the desk. Then he walked towards the locked door. The two MIBs picked up the comatose Leigh and carried her after him. Fishing a key from his jacket, Waverley unlocked the door and stood aside. They carried her through and it closed behind them. Beckoning his henchman to follow, Waverley swept out of the room.

Owen took his hand away from Eric's mouth. "Sorry, but I had to do that."

Eric nodded.

They waited a few seconds before cautiously emerging from the cupboard. Going to the desk, Owen took the hypo from its drawer and slipped it into his belt. "It could come in useful," he explained.

They approached the door Leigh had been taken through. As Owen suspected, Waverley hadn't locked it. He inched it open and looked down a flight of stairs. Their destination was shrouded in gloom. He turned to Eric and noted his grim expression. "Are you ready for this?"

"Yes."

"I'll go first." He inspected the wall around and inside the door. "There doesn't seem to be a light switch. But that's probably just as well. We don't want to advertise ourselves. Just a minute, though."

He went back to the desk and rifled through the drawers. In the bottom one he found a half-full box of safety matches. Passing Eric to get to the door, he brushed against the tape machine hanging from his shoulder. He'd forgotten about it.

"I'll take that now," he said.

"It's all right, I can manage."

"Better for me to have it. As they seem so anxious to get their hands on it, you'd probably be a target." He dug into his pocket for the tape. "And it makes sense to keep this in the machine." Owen took the recorder and loaded the cassette.

They began their descent. The stairwell was deep. They took it slowly, wary of surprises. Eventually it came to an end. Owen struck a match and held it up. A stone passage stretched ahead of them. The air smelt dank and fetid. He touched the wall. It was made of huge granite blocks which he guessed were very old. They were slimy with moss. The match flickered and died. He lit another.

"We'll keep our eyes open and mouths shut," he whispered. "And we've only got a few matches so we'll save them for when they're needed. OK?"

"OK."

The second match went out.

They moved into the darkness.

27

Poppy imagined that drowning was like this. She couldn't get any air into her lungs. Her eyes started to bulge and there was a growing pain in her chest. She was on the edge of surrendering to terrified panic.

For someone engaged in such a murderous attack, Saul's face was strangely passionless. She struggled to speak to him, but only managed a wheezing gasp. The room span and began to blur as he applied more pressure.

Fighting to get a grip on herself, she tried again. *"All ... right,"* she croaked, *"I'll ... tell ... you."*

Her words seemed to fall on deaf ears.

"If you ... don't ... stop ... you'll never ... find tape."

Slowly, his grip loosened. Then he let go and stepped back from her. "This had better not be a way of buying time."

Poppy took great gulps of air and rubbed her burning throat. "No ... no, it ... isn't, honestly. Owen ... *did* leave ... some tapes with ... me." Breathing more regularly now, she started to pull herself together. "The first ... one was ... music. I don't know what's on ... the other. Which do you ... want?"

"Both!"

"Okay. My office..."

He reached for her. She flinched. Taking her arm, he said, "Let's go and get them, shall we?"

Saul guided her out of the room. "Which way?" She nodded towards the reception area. He pushed her in front of him. They walked across the lobby and along another corridor. Thoughts of escape still filled her mind, but there was no opportunity to break away from him.

Her office was as chaotic as usual.

"Where?" he demanded.

"Give me a second to think."

He jerked her arm spitefully. She winced. "No, really! Look at the mess in here. I just need to remember exactly where —"

"Do it! And no tricks." He released her, but stayed close.

She sifted the piles of cassettes and CDs on her

desk, tossing them aside one after another. Saul was growing irritated. Finally, she found Owen's music tape.

"Here." She handed it to him and he put it in his pocket.

"Where's the other one?"

"Don't you want to play it?" she asked. "To check that —"

"*No!*"

The edge in his voice further confirmed her suspicion that he feared Owen's tapes. But why?

"Where is it?" he repeated.

"Er, it's back in the studio, come to think of it."

"Why didn't you tell me that before?"

"Sorry. Forgot. It's the sort of thing you're liable to do when someone's just tried to strangle you." She attempted a smile. It was weak.

He shoved her to the door. "Move."

On their way back, he wanted to know if she'd made any copies of the tapes. She lied, of course. "No. Why should I?"

"I do hope you're telling the truth, Ms Morgan."

Poppy thought that was rich, coming from him. And now it occurred to her that, once he'd got what he wanted, what was to stop him doing away with her anyway? If only because he must know she'd report all this.

As they arrived back at the studio, she decided that showing him there wasn't anything on the second tape might calm him down. So she led him directly to the heavy duty recording machine.

"Here you go," she said, hitting the play button. "It's blank. What's all the fuss about?"

Saul's face contorted with horror.

He screamed.

Owen thought about how hard it was to judge distance when you were walking in pitch blackness. And how easy to let your imagination get the better of you. He half-expected someone to leap at them. But the only sounds were his and Eric's muffled footfalls, and the occasional skittering of small stones their trainers kicked against.

Despite wanting to ration the matches, they used three in five minutes. Each short-lived burst of light was too weak to show the tunnel's end. Then, in the lead with a hand outstretched, Owen bumped into something. He struck another match, and found it was a metal door. Its sturdy lever-like handle refused to yield when he pushed down on it. The wall in which the door was set carried on to their right. But a further match revealed that this passage soon reached a dead end, forming an alcove. The only way forward was barred to them.

"That must have been where they took Leigh," Owen whispered. "Unless we passed somewhere else in the dark."

"What shall we do?" Eric asked.

"We could back-track and see if we missed another door, I suppose. But I don't think we did."

"What about going back up to the house?"

"Not if we can help it. It's too dangerous, and it won't get us to Leigh. Let's check that other passage more closely."

They went into the alcove and felt their way along the walls. But they got to the end without discovering anything.

"Well, it *was* a long shot," Owen admitted.

"Perhaps we should work our way back, like you said, and look for —"

Owen cut Eric short with an urgent "*Ssshhhh!*" A thin line of light had appeared at the edge of the door. It was opening.

They pressed themselves into the shadows as the two MIBs came out. One had a small torch. Luckily, he didn't point it in their direction as the men quickly hurried off along the tunnel.

Owen and Eric crept to the corner and watched the figures fade into the gloom. Then Owen turned to see the door slowly closing of its own accord. He grabbed Eric and pushed him in, then just managed to squeeze through the tightening gap himself. The door swung shut behind them with an echoing clang.

They were in a large, dimly lit, circular chamber. Crumbling granite pillars supported the roof and the floor was paved with flagstones. Owen guessed it was part of the abbey's original underground complex.

There were passageways leading out of the room's left- and right-hand sides. They took the left.

Before they got very far, the floor began to slope downwards, and the tunnel narrowed. It got darker, too, as they moved away from the chamber's lights. The air was musty.

Eventually they arrived at what looked like an entrance to another room, but couldn't see what was in it. Owen fumbled for a match. Its flame illuminated a mound of irregularly shaped, whitish objects. He stepped forward to make out what they were.

He faced a jumbled mass of yellowing human bones. A grinning skull sat on top of the gruesome heap. It clattered to one side, exposing the red-eyed, razor-toothed form of an enormous rat. Hissing, the rodent scurried from sight. Owen shuddered and backed off.

"I think they're very old," he told Eric. "This must be the abbey's catacombs, and those are probably the remains of generations of monks. There's no way through here." The match threatened to burn his fingers and he dropped it. "Come on," he said, "let's go back."

Returning to their starting point, they crossed to the right-hand tunnel. This one stayed level, and after two sharp corners it had soft lights in the ceiling. It took them to a door. There didn't seem to be a lock of any kind, and when Owen tried the handle it opened without difficulty.

They were dazzled by a brilliant glare.

A moment passed before their eyes adjusted to the room beyond. It was in complete contrast to everything they'd seen before. White and clean, it looked newly-built. Owen noticed that there were no visible light fixtures. The brightness was coming from the walls themselves. He ran his palm along one of them. It was cold, and consisted of a seamless, shiny covering that could have been plastic. Only he was sure it wasn't.

As they moved further in, they saw a large table, made of the same gleaming material. The objects laid out on it puzzled Owen greatly. There were twenty or thirty of them. Each was about the same shape and size as a rugby ball. They were muddy brown in colour.

Owen went over and touched one. It was quite smooth. He picked it up, and was surprised that it felt much heavier than it looked. As he held it, he became aware of two things. First, it was slightly warm. Second, and more disturbing, was a faint tingling sensation coming from it. It was similar to a mild electric shock and he found it unpleasant. He quickly put it down again.

Instinctively, he wiped his hands against the sides of his jeans, as though he had handled something ... *unwholesome*.

He realized Eric was standing beside him. "What the heck do you think these are?"

Eric shook his head.

Owen examined the rest of the strangely lumines-cent room. The only other thing in it appeared to be a machine of some sort. Again, it was fashioned from the unknown, glowing white substance. It consisted of an oblong box mounted on four tubular legs, and was approximately as tall as Owen. The face of the box displayed three rows of green and red lights that flashed on and off in a seemingly random pattern. But there were no visible controls of any kind, or any obvious power source.

Then Owen spotted the outline of another door on the far side of the room. It was set flush to the wall, and he could easily have missed it. There was no handle, or even a keyhole, so he tried pushing. It sprung inward.

A short corridor, made entirely of the glittery, not-quite plastic stuff stretched ahead. It went to an arched opening that seemed to promise yet another room. There being no other choice, they silently followed it. At its far end, Owen stepped through the curved entrance.

And was struck dumb with awe.

They were in a gigantic artificial cavern. The whole thing, from the floor to the domed roof far above, was constructed of the same glowing white substance. It was so vast Owen felt as insignificant as an ant in a football stadium. They drank in the spectacle word-lessly. Owen knew they couldn't afford the luxury of hanging around to gape at the place. He dragged his gaze away from the distant ceiling and began looking around on ground level.

About half-way across the immense expanse of floor, he saw a wall. As far as he could tell from this distance, it wasn't very high, and there were breaks in it to allow access to the other side. He started towards it, Eric trailing a few steps behind.

When they got there, the wall proved to be taller than they were. At least twice as tall. Mindful of the risk of running into someone, Owen cautioned Eric to keep quiet. Then he led them through the nearest breach.

For one crazy moment he thought they'd walked into a huge dormitory. What must have been thousands of low-lying couches spread out before them. They were in straight rows, spaced evenly apart, and stretched almost as far as they could see. The great majority were empty. But the ones far off, close to the opposite wall, looked as though they had people lying on them.

Owen glanced at Eric. His face was as expressionless as he imagined his own to be. The wonderment and sheer bizarreness of the sight must have sapped the emotion from their features.

They advanced.

As they got nearer to the reclining figures they realized there were hundreds of them. The first one Owen came to was a young woman. He didn't recognize her. She seemed to be in a perfectly natural state of sleep. But when he gently shook her, she didn't wake up. He did it again, a little more urgently, and she still didn't stir.

He moved on, scanning the acres of faces. Some seemed familiar. There, for instance, was a man who he was sure ran the bookshop in town. Near him, one of Leyswood's postmen, in a row adjacent to the cousin of somebody Owen went to school with. Grouped together on seven or eight of the couches were the journalists they'd seen at the roadblock. Next he stopped short on seeing Grace Harvey, the English teacher, and not far from her, Police Constable Andrews. He tried waking him, but again, there was no reaction.

Then Owen came upon Pete Collins, his usually brutish face softened by the calm of sleep. The following twenty or so people he hardly knew, if at all. But he couldn't fail to recognize George and Alice Pearce.

He looked around for Eric, saw him a dozen rows away and beckoned him over. Eric weaved his way to the spot and stared down at his aunt and uncle. Owen didn't know what to say, so he left him there and carried on scanning faces.

At the very end of the row he found Leigh.

He shook her harder than he had any of the others, and bent to whisper urgently in her ear. "Leigh. *Leigh!* It's me, Owen. Come on, wake up, Leigh!"

She couldn't be roused. Perhaps her brother would have more luck. As he lifted his arm to wave at Eric, Owen glanced down at the person on the first couch of the adjoining row.

It was his father.

28

Poppy didn't understand what was happening. Seconds before, she had feared for her life. Now the man she felt so threatened by looked as though he feared for his.

Ralph Saul's face was wreathed in dread. And agony.

Trembling right arm stretched out in front of him, he tottered weakly towards her. She thought he probably wouldn't make it, but retreated all the same.

Saul lifted his hands to the sides of his head and a hideous gurgling rose in his throat. His body spasmed and convulsed. He managed one more hesitant step before his legs gave way. Mouth gaping, eyes wild with terror, he plunged writhing to the floor.

It had to be the tape. There was no other explanation. *This* was why he was so desperately anxious to get it from her. And why Owen knew it to be so important.

She looked at it turning in the studio recording machine. It was spinning much more rapidly than it should. Then she realized that, in her terror, she'd forgotten to switch back from high-speed dub. The tape was in play mode, but set at a very fast rpm. Had there been anything audible on it, it would have sounded like a demented ice-cream van.

That also meant it was going to reach its end quickly. What would happen then? Or if she took pity on the pathetic, shuddering figure at her feet and stopped it? Would the effects wear off? Would he recover and menace her again? These thoughts vanished when she saw what was happening now.

Saul was changing.

Some kind of transformation was taking place as he twitched and thrashed and slobbered.

It was as though his body was casting off all appearance of humanity. And becoming ... something else. Something unclean. Something loathsome and disgusting. Something from a nightmare. A dreadful stench filled her nostrils. Revolted, she clamped a hand over her mouth and turned away, nauseated.

The Saul thing was steaming and sizzling as it mutated into another form. It was fantastic. Unbelievable. Such a horror didn't deserve to live. Poppy decided that if there was any chance of this monstrosity clinging to life because the tape ended, she'd play it again.

But she began to see she wouldn't have to.

He – *it* – was dying.

Stewart Carter was like all the others. He was in some kind of coma and couldn't be roused.

What was he doing here? Why were *any* of them here, sunk deep in their comatose states? Reluctantly, Owen moved on, checking face after face. Eric joined him.

They came across Mike Adams, the broadcaster, and Owen remembered that last time they'd seen him, in the back of the military truck. Somehow, he'd expected to find him here. And he wasn't at all surprised to discover the reclining figure of Ralph Saul. In fact, Owen was beginning to think there wasn't anything that could throw him now. He felt beyond being shocked.

He was wrong.

Four couches along, they found Ross Waverley.

How could that be? They'd just seen him up in the house. Why would he race down here ahead of them and . . . drug himself? Pretend to be asleep? But even without trying to wake him, Owen knew he wasn't pretending. If he thought that was the last of the shocks in store for him, he was wrong again.

Eric was lying in the next cot.

Astounded, Owen turned to face ... Eric. The Eric standing beside him. The *real* Eric. Or ... Confusion was not a strong enough word to describe what Owen was feeling. He looked at the peacefully sleeping Eric. Then at the one he'd arrived with. The Eric at his side twisted his mouth into a malicious smile.

Owen's blood ran cold.

The false Eric's face hardened and became a picture of icy triumph. Owen saw nothing but evil there. And was afraid.

"Ah. Young Mr Carter. How nice of you to pay us a visit."

Owen spun at the sound of an all too familiar voice. He was confronted by Waverley. Leigh stood next to him.

Another Waverley. Another Leigh.

Brain reeling, he gaped at them.

"It's here," Eric told them smugly. "In the machine." He pointed at the tape recorder hanging from Owen's shoulder.

Betrayed.

A grim-looking MIB appeared, strode over and wrenched it from him. Owen was too dazed to resist. The man handed the machine to Waverley, who flipped it open to check the tape was inside. Then he placed the recorder on an empty couch beside him. Owen gave the imposter who called himself Eric a look of contempt. Waverley saw it. "Yes," he sneered, "he is with us."

The phoney Leigh spoke. "It's the end of your little adventure, Owen Carter," she said coldly.

"Restrain him!" Waverley snapped. "We'll prepare him now."

As the MIB reached for Owen, he remembered the hypodermic gun tucked in his belt. He jerked himself to one side, dragged it out and shoved it into the man's chest. Once, twice, three times he pulled the trigger. He heard the ping and hiss as each dose of tranquillizer penetrated flesh. He squeezed again and again until the shots were all used up. The man in black didn't pass out, collapse or react in any way. He simply folded his arms and regarded Owen with scorn.

"Oh, really," Waverley mocked, "you'll have to do better than *that*. Seize him!"

Poppy had to keep a clear head and not allow the shock to get to her. She fought against the urge to panic. Running around like a headless chicken wasn't going to help.

Avoiding sight of the squirming obscenity on the studio floor, she tried to think rationally. When she had a problem, she often found it was best solved by breaking it down into its component parts. OK. This was only another problem, she told herself. Bizarre, incredible, almost beyond belief, but still just a problem. And she could solve it.

What were the facts? First: the person she thought of as Professor Ralph Saul wasn't a person at all. She didn't know *what* he was, but that was beside the point at the moment.

Second: Owen's tape was killing him. Or it, rather.

A pool of viscous green liquid began oozing from the writhing body. And she knew she was only doing this to stop herself going insane.

She breathed deeply. Right. Third: when Saul was still Saul, so to speak, he implied that there were others like him. The thought sent goosebumps up her spine. Therefore, she persisted, Owen's tape should affect them the same way. Poppy was quite pleased with this little exercise in logic. Now, how was she going to use what she'd come up with?

You *idiot*! she thought. You're in a *radio station*!

She set to work connecting the high-speed copying machine containing Owen's deadly tape to the machine next to it. Then she put two blank tapes in the second machine. Now she needed Owen's music tape.

It was in Saul's pocket. Well, the *original* was. Of course she hadn't told him it was 525's policy to make copies of everything they intended broadcasting. She got the copy from a shelf on the far side of the room. This went into the first machine's other slot. It took her five minutes to mix both of Owen's tapes together, making sure the "silent" one was high-speed. She made two copies and dropped one into her handbag on the desk. She put the other on a continuous loop and pitched it through the mixing board. Then she substituted it for whatever was being broadcast at the moment.

Poppy had turned Radio 525 FM into a lethal weapon. Lethal to any of Saul's kind that happened to hear it, that is.

She hoped they liked music.

Anybody else listening to the station – anybody "normal" – would just hear Owen's demo tape and not be aware of the second recording beneath it.

It seemed like a good idea to take a few precautions to make the building itself secure. She piped the tape through the internal speakers. That meant it could be heard in both studios, all the offices and the reception area. In theory, the place should be impossible for any of Saul's friends, whatever they might be, to enter.

Next, she switched everything to 525's own emergency generator, in case they tried cutting off the electricity supply.

Then she remembered how the station signal had been swamped by interference recently. But there wasn't anything she could do about that except trust to luck.

Grabbing her bag, and tiptoeing carefully around the heaving thing on the floor, she ran to her office.

She came back with the keys and a tube of superglue for the studio lock. If that little lot didn't slow them down, nothing would.

In reception, she tried ringing the police, but still couldn't get the dialling tone. She decided to drive to the police station.

The sun had risen by this time, although the streets outside were still deserted.

But as she walked into the car park, she saw a young man lounging by the gate. He was massively built, wore a tatty leather jacket and had his hair in a ponytail. When he saw her he took his hands out of his pockets and called, "Poppy Morgan?"

He came over to her. She didn't like the look of him.

"Who wants to know?" she said.

"I'm a mate of Owen Carter's. He sent me to get you. Said it's really urgent, and to be sure you came."

"What did you say your name was?" Poppy asked again.

"Oh, yeah, sorry. Pete. Pete Collins."

It was like a dream. Except Owen knew he wasn't going to wake up. The MIB had him in an armlock. And the beings who looked identical to Waverley, Eric and Leigh gloated at him.

"Who are you?" Owen said. "*What* are you?"

"Haven't you guessed yet, Carter?" Waverley said. "And to think you're probably one of the brighter examples of your species."

Species? Owen thought.

"You look puzzled," Waverley continued smugly. "Yet the truth is quite simple. We are from ... *beyond* your planet."

"You're –" Owen faltered.

"Comprehension begins to dawn in your dim brain at last."

"But ... *what* are you?"

"You could not begin to understand. Even the name of our race would mean nothing to you. The universe is unimaginably vast, and we have travelled for far longer than you can comprehend. Our entire history is one of constant movement, seeking planets to provide us with ... sustenance."

Owen didn't like the sound of that. "But why the secrecy? Why not come openly and —"

Waverley snorted derisively. "That is not our way! We do not co-operate, we conquer! We do not ask, we take! And we are going to take your world, Owen Carter, just as we have taken so many before."

"And sucked them dry, no doubt! That's why you have to keep moving on, isn't it? You're nothing but parasites!"

"We are proud to be called such."

Owen remembered the spherical, tingling objects he'd found. "Of course! How could I be so dumb? Those things falling from the sky –"

"Are both part of us and our mode of transport."

"But they're so small. How –"

"Don't be fooled by appearances. We are not as you see us now. When we move through space it is in an embryonic, gaseous form. Upon discovering another species, we assume its guise."

"You can change *shape*..."

"We adapt," the Eric thing said, "using organic life forms as models." He slapped his chest with his palm. "This is but a façade. Our true appearance is very ... different."

"What happens to the races you copy?" Owen asked.

Waverley said, "The process of duplication takes a while to complete. Our hosts must be kept alive during this period to assure success."

"I don't understand."

"There is a link between each of us and the individual we model ourselves on. It cannot be broken until we have fully attuned ourselves to their likeness." Waverley swept an arm to indicate the sleeping forms surrounding them. "During the period of transference, which can take several of your weeks, their fate and ours is closely bound together. So we must keep them safely, in a trance state, until the time comes to dispose of them."

"*Kill* them, you mean," Owen said darkly.

Waverley ignored him. "In fact, in the case of humans we have improved upon the original. These pseudo-bodies we inhabit can regenerate when necessary. Thus bullets, for example, have no lasting effect on us, as I believe you discovered. We are virtually indestructible!"

The duplicate of Leigh said, "We're wasting time. He should be prepared without delay."

"Yes," the Waverley clone agreed. He addressed the MIB. "Bring what is needed."

The man let go of Owen and strode off towards the entrance tunnel.

Frightened as he was, there were still questions Owen wanted answering. Massaging the numbness from his arm, he said, "Why here? Leyswood, I mean."

The pseudo-Eric answered. "It has the advantage of being a fairly small and isolated community. That makes it easier for us to control. When we have succeeded here, we will move on to a full-scale invasion of the planet."

"A dress rehearsal," Owen whispered.

"We took the essential people first," Waverley explained. "The police, power workers..." That explained Turner, Owen's neighbour, who worked for the electricity company. "... and, most importantly, key personnel in communications. Which means we can manipulate telephone lines and so on to our advantage. And Ross Waverley's media empire has been particularly useful as a propaganda tool."

"You've been interfering with the signal from his radio station."

"Yes, and any other radio or TV broadcast that can be received in this town. Blocking Leyswood from the outside world has obvious advantages for us."

"How do you do it?"

"Very simply, with the level of technology at our command. In fact, you passed the device we use on your way in here."

Owen assumed he meant the odd machine in the glowing chamber. He decided to push his luck and try for a few more answers. "My dad, and Leigh's aunt and uncle – why take them over?"

"Your father, as a university lecturer, gave us access to the academic world. George Pearce's standing in the business community has proved valuable in helping us infiltrate commerce."

"We saw people being transported in the back of a military truck. I suppose they were your . . . victims?"

"Precisely. Important locals, people in positions of power and influence, being brought here to be replaced."

"But how did you manage to involve the army?"

"We didn't," Waverley said. "We simply located some military uniforms. It didn't take us long to realize how obedient your race is when confronted by the trappings of authority."

"What about Ralph Saul?"

"So many questions!" the alien leader mocked. "Curiosity seems to be another hallmark of your species. We took Saul not only for his importance in scientific circles, but because he had begun to guess the truth. In fact, we got to him just in time."

Owen glanced at the retreating MIB. "And you needed some muscle, of course, for the really dirty work."

"Indeed. Our enforcers have proved invaluable. Young Peter Collins is an outstanding example."

"Yeah, a bully. Just like you!" Owen spat.

The thing that looked like Waverley smiled. Cruelly.

Poppy didn't trust this Collins character. With the memory of Saul still horribly fresh in her mind, she couldn't afford to trust anybody. But suppose he really was a friend of Owen's, and could take her to him?

"Where *is* Owen?" she asked.

"He's at my place, over by the new estate. It won't take long in your car."

"What about his other friends? Leigh and Eric?"

"Er, yeah, they're there as well. They're waiting for us."

It didn't ring true. But she couldn't be entirely sure. Then she realized there was a little test she could put Collins through. One that would tell her if he was similar in . . . *nature* to Ralph Saul.

"OK," she said. "Let's go." They headed for her car. She unlocked and held open the passenger door for Collins. "In you get," she told him. "And don't forget the seat-belt."

Poppy opened the driver's door while he crammed in his bulk. She waited until he adjusted the belt and clicked it into place. Leaning in, she said, "You don't mind a little music, do you?" He shrugged.

Poppy was glad she always kept the car radio tuned to 525. She snapped it on.

Owen's music was drowned by the youth's agonized screams.

One look at what was happening to him was enough. She hurriedly backed away. How many of the damned things *were* there?

And what was she going to do now? She could hardly use her car with *that* thrashing around inside it. The same putrid smell that had come from the dying Saul began drifting over to her.

Poppy ran back into the building. Luckily, the drawer behind the receptionist's desk wasn't locked, and she retrieved a bunch of keys from it. One of them was for the company car.

She had wheels again.

All Owen could do was play for time. Not that he thought it would do him much good. This was one fix he couldn't see a way out of.

"How long has Eric been ... one of you?" he asked.

Confusingly, it was the "new" Eric who replied. "Since we caught him at the roadblock. Then it was my job to get you to the school basement to be captured."

"Didn't work, did it?"

"Didn't it? You're here, aren't you?"

Owen didn't have an answer to that one.

Waverley added, "We were concerned you would have noticed a change in your friend, despite intensively briefing his duplicate. And he was under strict orders to do nothing to give himself away until you were in our hands. But it was a risk; it can take us a while to become used to an unfamiliar culture.''

''That's why my father was acting so strange, right?'' Owen said. ''Or what I thought was my father. And Ralph Saul and Grace Harvey and all the rest of them.''

''Yes. But we learn quickly. In time, there would be absolutely no way of telling us from your own kind.''

The MIB had reappeared at the far side of the cavernous room. He was carrying what looked like a tray. Owen knew he had just minutes left. ''Would I be right in saying you wanted my tape so badly because it could make you ill?''

''Under certain circumstances, much more than simply ill,'' Waverley responded. ''It posed quite a threat to us.''

''How?''

''When we are in our embryonic state, nothing can harm us. But we are vulnerable during the period of transition. What you blundered into, with your incredibly primitive technology, was a tone that matched the vibration rate of our sub-molecular structure. In other words, it could shake loose that link between ourselves and our hosts. And once the link is severed, we cease to exist.''

''You mean die?''

''We are terminated, yes. Fortunately, your

recording was made at less than the optimum speed and merely caused us discomfort. But you could have discovered this at any time and adjusted it."

"If me and my friends were such a problem for you, why didn't you just kill us?"

"We are wasting time!" the Leigh clone hissed.

"He isn't going anywhere," the Waverley thing told her. He turned back to Owen. "We had to be sure of obtaining the tape, along with any copies you might have made. Also, we're not completely in control yet. The repercussions of three murdered teenagers could have been unfortunate. No, it's much better that you be replaced."

The MIB was getting nearer. And it *was* a tray he was carrying, although Owen couldn't see what was on it. He could make a guess though.

"None of that is of any importance now," Waverley said. "The threat is eliminated. And soon we will be numerous enough to come out into the open."

"What happens then?"

"Your race will be overwhelmed, of course. Some will be spared, temporarily, to act as slaves. They will be put to work refashioning this planet to suit our needs. Regrettably, the new environment's atmosphere will be unsuitable for human life. But we shall be able to revert to our true forms. Eventually, we will move on."

"Don't count on it!" Owen raged. "The human race doesn't give in that easily!"

"If I were capable of having what you call a sense of humour," Waverley informed him, "I expect I would find that quite funny."

The MIB reached the group. There was one of the oval objects and a hypo gun on the tray he carried. "Proceed," Waverley ordered.

"Leigh" placed the sphere at Owen's feet while the MIB grabbed him. "Waverley" took the hypo gun.

"What a pity you will not be here to see the new world we are about to create," he said.

He advanced, the hypodermic raised. There was a rasping sound. Owen looked down and saw a crack running across the surface of the sphere. A gush of foul-smelling green gas spurted out.

He struggled, but it was futile. The flow of gas increased, forming a damp, thickening cloud.

And it began to take on a shape.

Owen's shape.

The stinking green cloud swirled in front of him. Owen twisted and heaved, but couldn't get away from the MIB's steely grip. Stern-faced, the Waverley alien approached, hypodermic gun levelled.

It was the end. Owen was finished. He closed his eyes and waited for oblivion.

A loud groan sounded somewhere to their right.

Owen opened his eyes again and saw the others looking in the direction of the noise. Another groan came, louder and deeper than before. Something moved in the centre of the mass of slumbering bodies.

Waverley curtly nodded at the duplicate Eric and Leigh. They ran towards the commotion.

Someone out there was sitting up. And moaning.

"It cannot be," Waverley hissed. "Unless..."

Then a gasping shriek rang out, quite close to hand. Another figure was stirring just two rows away. Owen recognized the unmistakable, burly frame of Pete Collins.

Waverley murmured, "They must have been terminated."

He couldn't mean Collins and the other awakened sleeper. It had to be the aliens *impersonating* them. Somehow they'd died and released their human hosts from bondage.

"See to it!" Waverley barked at the MIB. "I'll take care of this one."

Owen's captor released him and sprinted off to deal with Collins. At the same time, the turmoil at the point where the first person had woken up increased. Owen thought the man struggling with the synthetic Leigh and Eric could have been Ralph Saul. Waverley's attention was divided between this unexpected turn of events and Owen. It was a moment of utter confusion.

And a heaven-sent opportunity.

Owen took it. He balled his fist and aimed a blow, not at Waverley, but at the hypo gun in his hand. His knuckles connected with it in a stinging crack and the instrument flew from the alien's grasp. Then Owen dived to one side, missing the spiralling green cloud by a hair's breadth. He hit the floor awkwardly, but ignored the pain and scrambled to his feet. Waverley roared something unintelligible.

Owen dashed for the only thing that might save his life. The tape recorder. He smashed into the couch it was lying on. Instantly, Waverley was upon him, arms around his waist in a breath-crushing bear hug. But Owen had the machine in his trembling hands. He jabbed the play button.

The alien gasped as though he'd been struck in the stomach by a prize fighter. He let go, reeled and collided with the couch behind him.

As Owen turned to run, several images impressed themselves upon him. Even from this distance, he could see that the other aliens were affected by the tape, too. The MIB at Collins' side had his hands clamped over his ears and was going down. The Eric and Leigh clones were doubling up in agony.

And the loathsome green cloud was beginning to melt away.

Owen remembered what "Waverley" had said about the tape. It needed to be played at a higher speed to do them real damage. As there was no way the portable tape machine's speed could be increased, it had only limited use as a weapon. They could recover at any time.

He wanted to go to Saul and Collins, and lead them out of the place. But he saw they were only half conscious and babbling with delirium. They would have to take care of themselves. It was a hard decision, and Owen felt a stab of conscience. But, armed with the knowledge he'd gained, he had some small chance of helping them all.

If he could get out of this hell hole in one piece.

Slinging the tape machine over his shoulder, he sprinted for the corridor, expecting hordes of aliens to emerge and grab him at any second. He reached the entrance unmolested.

Panting, he rushed along the tunnel, through the door and into the white room. When he saw the table, he grasped its edge and upended it, sending the alien space eggs scattering in all directions.

It probably wouldn't do them any harm but it made him feel better.

Then he noticed the machine that Waverley said blocked TV and radio transmissions. He quickly grabbed the table and, holding it like a battering ram, smashed it into the apparatus. There was a muffled bang, a shower of blue sparks exploded from the machine's face and its lights went out.

A second later Owen was through the door and pounding down the tunnel leading to the ancient chamber. Still he met no other aliens and prayed his luck would hold.

A stitch in his side, fighting for air, he reached the pitch-black corridor that connected with the stairs to the house. He scraped his arms and legs against the walls in his anxiety to get to the end of it. Once, he tripped, and narrowly avoided falling headlong to the stone floor.

There was a clanging noise from the rear. He looked back and saw the flickering yellow beams of flashlights.

They were after him.

Lungs flaming, he went up the staircase on all fours, clawing at the steps for purchase. The door to Waverley's study was before him. He rose to his feet, head swimming with exertion, and flung it open.

Two MIBs were in the room. One stood by the antique desk. The other had just come in through the French windows. They started towards Owen. He thumbed the volume slide of the cassette machine to maximum. The men stopped dead in their tracks, eyes widened with shock, mouths agape from pain. The first collapsed across the desk, strewing telephone, pens and a stack of books. The second jerked back, sagged and pitched to the floor.

Heavy footfalls sounded on the staircase. Owen dashed for the French windows, leaping over the convulsive legs of the MIB, and scooted out to the path.

When he reached the front of the house he had the terrible thought that the gates might have been closed. But as he sprinted along the drive, scattering pebbles, he saw they were still open. Angry voices rang out behind him.

He pelted across the open ground and into the trees where he and the fake Eric had hidden earlier.

Casting a quick glance over his shoulder, he saw figures pouring out of the gates. It occurred to him that the recorder's batteries could be near to exhaustion. And how would he know they'd run out if the tape was silent? He shut it off to conserve them.

Deep into the thicket now, he made for the track. His pursuers plunged into the bushes to the rear of him. He came to the spot where the motorbike was parked and began tearing at the foliage covering it. The MIBs were close. Almost close enough to be seen. Leaves rustled and branches snapped. They'd be upon him any second.

Owen fished the ignition key out of his sock and shakily inserted it. He clambered astride the machine, clicked on the engine and walloped his foot on the starter.

The motor turned over once, coughed and died.

He'd given away his position now and they were hacking through the trees towards him.

He kicked the starter again. The engine turned over once more. And once more fell silent.

A man in black smashed through the bushes. Owen was torn between turning the recorder back on or giving the bike another try. He decided on the bike first. The MIB lurched towards him, his face murderous.

Grimly clutching the handlebars, Owen bore

down on the starter as hard as he could. The engine spluttered, sparked and roared into throbbing life. He bumped on to the track and left the gesticulating man behind.

To Owen's right, a jeep was bouncing out of the house. He swerved left, in the direction of the Leyswood road. He was just beginning to pick up speed when another MIB leapt out of the under-growth in front of him. The man stood in the middle of the track, barring his way, frantically waving his arms.

Owen hit him.

It was a glancing blow, but still sent the man flying to the verge like a tossed rag doll, limbs splayed.

At the main highway, Owen contemplated turning right and trying to get through the roadblocks. Then he saw a convoy of vehicles speeding at him from that direction. He turned left.

Throttle wide open, he thundered towards Leyswood.

The motorcycle's shrieking engine knifed through the early morning silence. Crisp, rushing air whipping his face, Owen looked back. At least three cars were following him. The two in front were jeeps. Waverley's limousine was behind them.

The bike's speedometer nudged seventy. Owen leaned into the wind, willing the machine to go faster. In his mirror, he saw the leading jeep put on a burst of speed and begin to eat up the distance between them. Within seconds it was near enough for him to see it was crowded with MIBs.

One of them was leaning out of the passenger window.

He pointed something. There was a *crack* and the sound of breaking glass. The light on the back of the bike had shattered, peppering the road with a trail of shards.

They were shooting at him.

He hadn't thought about them having guns. If they hit a tyre, or got near enough to hit *him*, it was all over.

Another bullet zinged over his left shoulder. He ducked and tried to make himself a harder target by weaving from one side of the road to the other. He came to a bend and rounded it without dropping speed. For a second, the pursuing vehicles were lost from sight.

Then the leading jeep skidded around the corner. It was gaining. The MIB got off two more shots in quick succession. They were wide of their mark. Owen adopted the evasive, weaving action again. In his mirror, the jeep was near enough for him to see the faces of the driver and gunman. At least the alien had stopped firing now. But the jeep was no more than two lengths behind. The motorbike's speedo registered eighty. It was flat out. There was nothing left to give.

The jeep drew level on the outside. Owen looked across at the open passenger window and understood why the MIB wasn't firing. He was reloading his revolver. Owen had to think fast. At this range he didn't stand a chance.

He had an idea. It was desperate. Insane. But so was the situation.

He edged the speeding bike as near to the jeep as he dared. Then he took his left hand off the handlebars and slid the tape recorder's strap down his arm. One-handed, he thumbed the play button.

The MIB finished loading the gun, looked up, took aim.

It was now or never.

Owen flung the cassette machine at him and pulled away. It spun through the air and into the open window. He had the fleeting impression of the MIB entangled with the recorder and its lashing strap. The alien's mouth formed a gaping, terrified "O". Beyond him, the driver let go of the steering wheel and clamped his hands to his face.

Out of control, the jeep veered across the lanes and on to the verge. It ploughed through a wooden fence and plunged over the embankment. There was a tremendous explosion. A huge orange fireball erupted from the tumbling vehicle. Owen glanced into the mirror and saw the jeep wreathed in flames. A pall of oily black smoke was beginning to rise. Then he sped around another corner, and the scene disappeared from sight.

One less. But now his only sure defence against them had gone.

In the distance, something was approaching. Owen squinted and saw it was a large removal truck. He checked the mirror. The other jeep and the limo were getting nearer. He figured that an argument between the oncoming truck and either of the cars behind him was unlikely to hurt the truck very much. And if he did what he had in mind properly, the truck driver shouldn't be harmed. Owen just hoped he had the necessary nerve.

Holding his breath, he steered into the right-hand side of the road, directly in the truck's path. Its driver sounded his horn. Owen stayed in the wrong lane. The truck grew bigger. Limousine and jeep were closing the gap. The furniture truck's horn sounded again. Owen could read the name of the company painted above the cab now. He had to get it exactly right and give the driver enough time to brake. The horn became one continuous high-pitched note. And the driver's horrified face was clearly visible.

Owen swerved back into the correct lane. But not before the lorry driver had applied his brakes and spun the steering wheel.

The huge truck skewed across both lanes. It turned in a great arc, and came to a juddering halt with its nose pointed at one side of the road and its tail the other. It was a barrier now. A wall of metal in the path of the approaching cars.

The jeep ran straight into it with a shattering explosion of glass and steel.

Whoever – *whatever* – was driving the limo had quicker reactions. It screeched through a gap between the back end of the truck and the roadside fence. And kept coming.

Owen saw the tiny figure of the truck driver climb out of his cab and wave his fist at him.

The outskirts of town lay ahead. A quick look in the mirror showed the limo still on his tail, but further back than before. Houses began dotting the sides of the road, and some Saturday morning traffic was visible. He would have to reduce speed. What he was going to do when he got into Leyswood, he didn't know. All he could think of was dumping the bike somewhere and looking for a place to hide.

Suburban streets flashed past. There were people walking the pavements. More cars were about. Five minutes would bring him to the centre, and crowds of early shoppers.

Owen crossed an intersection. After he passed, a police car turned out of it and started to trail him. He accelerated. The panda car's siren wailed and its flashing lights came on. He began turning corners at random to shake them off.

The next time he looked, the police car and Waverley's limo had been joined by yet another jeep. Quite a little procession. Fortunately, the greater flexibility of the motorcycle kept him ahead of them.

They were nearer the centre of town. Despite being a built-up area, he risked more speed, trusting in his skill to help him avoid crashing.

Then he noticed a white station wagon coming towards him on the other side of the road. He recognized the driver. It was Poppy Morgan.

Their eyes met as they passed. And Owen took in a slogan on the side of her car reading *Radio 525 FM – The Home of Modern Music.*

She hit her brakes, executed a three-point turn and tagged on to the end of the convoy.

At the front of the line, Owen saw something strange. A Telecom van was parked at the side of the road with its back doors open. A small crowd of people were looking at it from a distance. As he flew past, he saw two men lying on the pavement. At least one of them was having some kind of fit.

Aliens! They *had* to be. But how had they been exposed to his tape?

Poppy saw it too, and knew what must have happened. She returned her attention to the chase.

Heads turned as the bizarre collection of vehicles shot by. People pointed. One or two waved, probably thinking the limousine contained a VIP, accompanied by an escort.

At the corner of the High Street a car had crashed into a lamppost. Its door hung open and a woman thrashed and twisted in the driving seat. Again, there was a baffled-looking crowd, watching from a safe distance. By now, Owen had put two and two together. The only other copy of his tape he knew about was the one he gave Poppy. He guessed she'd been clever with it.

If only the aliens chasing him would turn on *their* car radios.

Here in the heart of town the evidence of Poppy's work was everywhere. A shopkeeper convulsed at the entrance to his dry cleaning store, a semi-circle of appalled spectators goggling at him. Every few yards, knots of people surrounded fallen figures on the pavement, and even in the road itself. There was an occasional scream. The most macabre sight was of a window cleaner, his foot caught in a rung, hanging upside-down from his ladder. He spasmed and shrieked as puzzled on-lookers fretted. A small transistor radio stood next to his bucket on a window sill.

Poppy didn't know if Owen realized his tape actually killed these monsters pretending to be people. She wondered how long it would be before widespread panic set in among the human population.

Owen didn't know if Poppy realized what she was seeing were really aliens. He thought it was only a matter of time before people started panicking.

By the front door of the public library a man in a jogging suit was on his knees, desperately trying to disentangle himself from a Walkman. The dramas Owen was passing had briefly taken his concentration away from the road. Now he looked ahead and saw a single-decker bus pulling out of a side street and into his path. It was no coincidence. *They* were boxing him in. That left him only one option.

He wrenched hard left on the handlebars, bounced over the kerb and on to the pavement. People

scattered and pressed themselves into shop door-
ways. Angry cries rose in his wake. He didn't want to
hit anyone, but it took every ounce of his ability not
to.

Poppy watched this from her position at the back of
what was now a queue of traffic. She guessed Owen
would get himself on to the road again at the next
corner he came to. Having just passed a turning, she
decided to reverse to it. Hopefully, she'd be able to
catch up with him.

Owen zigzagged through the pedestrians, causing
several of them to drop their shopping. He narrowly
missed a display of potted plants outside a florist's.
Then he reached a corner, left the pavement with a
jolt and rejoined the road.

He was leaving the heart of town now. If he kept
going in this direction he would have eventually
crossed the whole of Leyswood. But there were no
major roads on the other side, just walkers' paths
through the moorland. The motorbike was much
heavier than the scramblers he was used to, and he
didn't think it would take the terrain.

But at least he seemed to have lost the aliens
chasing him.

It was too hasty a judgement. The police car
reappeared two blocks ahead. Then the jeep and the
limo. He tore past the imposing façade of the parish
church. The wail of the police siren grew louder.

Two blocks later they entered the town's industrial

section. Small factories and warehouses spread out on either side. Ahead, the road wound around a field before reaching Leyswood's shopping mall. Beyond that, there was only open moor.

There was hardly any traffic here at the weekend and the chase picked up speed. Owen leaned into the road's first bend. Then he straightened out and prepared to take the next.

He went into it too fast. The bike wobbled. He squeezed the brakes, but harder and later than he should. He felt himself losing balance. The motorcycle bucked, skidded and pitched to its side.

Owen was thrown off.

He thudded to the tarmac, rolled several times and lay still.

32

He must have knocked his head and passed out. But it couldn't have been for long. The bike was on its side in the middle of the road, the front wheel slowly spinning. And he could hear the police siren approaching. He was lying on the grass verge, which had cushioned his fall. There didn't seem to be any broken bones, just a soreness in his right leg, and his palms were grazed. He'd been lucky.

He nearly laughed. *Lucky?* With carloads of homicidal aliens about to arrive? *Some luck.*

He struggled to his feet. The leg was stiff and he felt unsteady. His hands shook.

A pool of oil spread from the overturned motorcycle. It was a write-off.

The siren grew louder. He had to get away from

here. But where could he go? There were two choices. Either he carried on along this road until he got to the moor, or he headed for the shopping mall. The road offered no cover. It had to be the mall. He began limping over the field towards it.

Before he was half-way across, the pursuing cars appeared. He saw them slow down at the spot where the bike lay. They must have seen him, but carried on along the road, gathering speed. Owen was sure they knew he had only one place to go and would try to cut him off. Ignoring the pain in his leg, he started to run. Reaching a low fence, he scrambled over into the mall's car park. There was no sign of the police car, jeep or limo yet. He jogged in the direction of the red brick and glass building.

There were quite a few people about. Mums and dads, toddlers, babies in prams, shoppers pushing laden trolleys. Everything seemed so ordinary and normal. Taking a quick look behind before going through the main entrance, he saw the police car draw up. The siren and lights had been switched off. Three uniformed officers jumped out. Owen put his head down and went in. The sight of the milling throng, the smell of fast food, the piped muzak all assaulted his senses.

His plan was to get to the other side of the immense ground floor and out the back exit. To avoid attracting attention, he walked rather than ran.

It was hard. He never felt more like running in his life.

As he made his way through the jostling crowd, one thought was constantly in his mind. *Which of the innocent-looking people around him weren't really people at all?*

A group of young men swaggered from a burger bar and gave him stern looks. Were they human? What about the woman dragging her protesting child into a shoe shop? The middle-aged man at the counter of the travel agent's? The pair of teenage girls flipping through CDs outside the record store? Or the old lady who seemed more interested in him than the book she was holding? He imagined every eye in the place was directed his way.

At least, he hoped he imagined it.

When he got to the back door he saw the jeep parked outside and quickly turned away. All he could do now was go up.

He moved briskly to the escalators. As the moving stairs carried him to the next floor he scanned the scene below. He saw someone in black clothing, so out of place in the heat, approaching two security guards. The MIB spoke to them for a moment and they all walked off in different directions. He watched as one of the guards went to a man sitting on a bench. After a brief conversation, the man got up and they parted. Then the man stopped a woman pushing a shopping basket and talked with her.

They were spreading the word.

Just before the escalator levelled out, he caught a glimpse of Alice and George Pearce, and several of the journalists from the roadblock. To be accurate, he saw things that *looked* like them.

One whole wall on the first floor was made of glass. Owen went over and found it gave him a view of the car park. The Eric, Leigh and Waverley duplicates were walking towards the entrance, located under the window. The alien Eric looked up and saw him. Owen cursed himself for being so stupid. But it was too late. They'd all seen him now and were dashing into the building.

Desperately, he looked for somewhere to hide.

Poppy had been lucky to find the cars chasing Owen again. She very nearly lost them in the back streets. Now she sat in the station wagon outside the mall. She was watching Waverley, and Owen's friends, Leigh and Eric.

Assuming they really *were* Owen's friends. And not something else.

She saw them walking towards the centre's entrance. Then Eric stopped and pointed to the window above. Poppy looked up and saw Owen there. The way they ran into the place made her think they weren't Owen's friends at all. And they *had* got out of one of the cars that had chased him here. She decided to treat them as hostile.

Grabbing her bag, she left the station wagon and followed them.

She saw a policeman near the main door. Her first thought was to go to him and ask for help. But she remembered how a police car had been one of the vehicles chasing Owen too. This officer could have been in it. Her experience with the monsters calling themselves Saul and Collins had made her suspicious of everyone. She decided not to talk to him. Just in case.

Inside, Poppy was in time to see Waverley and the others elbowing their way up the escalator. Her instinct was to follow. But she'd made a stupid mistake when she left the studio. She had forgotten to bring a cassette machine. And the tape in her bag was useless as a weapon if she couldn't play it.

Simple. She'd buy one. A shopping mall, of all places, would sell tape recorders. Only, she had to move fast, and hope Owen could stay out of their way.

Then she realized something. And had a *much* better idea.

Owen found the fire exit. There was a beefy security man guarding it.

He'd almost completed a circuit of the floor, looking for another way out, when he saw "Waverley" barging up the escalator. "Leigh" and

"Eric" were right behind him. Owen slipped into a china shop and pretended to browse.

Getting himself behind an open plan display of glass ornaments, he watched the aliens split up and begin searching for him. Then his eye was drawn back to the top of the escalator. Constable Andrews was stepping off it, alongside Mike Adams. They were followed by Grace Harvey and a couple of the journalists.

For all Owen knew, *everybody* coming up could have been non-human. They must have put out some kind of general alert and brought in as many of their kind as possible. It was an all-out effort to get Owen. But if he was right in thinking that Poppy had managed to broadcast his tape, they probably knew about it by now. They couldn't be *that* dumb. No, their only motivation had to be pure revenge.

They wanted to kill him.

The china shop's sales assistant eyed him suspiciously. She might have thought he was a shoplifter. Or it could have been more sinister. He edged to the door. Stepping outside, he turned left.

And stared death in the face.

The sign read *Manager's Office*. Poppy didn't bother knocking. A portly man in a cheap suit sat behind a desk. On the other side of the room a young, heavily made-up blonde woman pounded a keyboard.

The man looked up and said, "Excuse me, but this

is a private area. No admittance to members of the public."

"Are you the manager?" Poppy asked.

"If you have a complaint, there is a correct procedure to follow."

"No. I don't want to complain, it's just —"

"Complaints department, second floor. Thank you."

"Like I said, I don't want to complain –"

He got up. "Then I'm afraid I shall have to ask you to leave."

"*Look*," Poppy said, growing irritated, "this is an emergency and —"

"First aid? Lost children? Both ground floor, at the rear. Good morning."

To heck with it, she thought. Poppy stuck her hand in her jacket pocket, extended her fingers and pointed the bulge at him. "*Don't move!*" she said. "I've got a gun and I'm prepared to use it!"

The blonde woman gave a little squeak and covered her mouth. The manager sat down again and swallowed.

"Keep quiet and you won't get hurt!"

"What do you ... want? Mo ... mo ... money?" the manager stammered.

"No." She jabbed her empty pocket at the blonde. "You. Where's the Tannoy system?" The woman looked blank. "The thing you play the *music* through," Poppy explained.

Trembling, the woman indicated a large wooden box with knobs and switches on it.

"Is there a radio attached?"

She nodded.

"I want you to tune to Radio 525 and patch it through the speakers."

The manager and his secretary looked at each other, mystified.

"*Now!*" Poppy barked.

"Do as she says, Doreen," the manager said. "She's obviously mad."

Waverley seemed almost as surprised to see Owen as Owen was to see him. For a second, they stared at each other. Then Owen turned and ran for his life.

He belted past three or four shops, the alien in hot pursuit, and came to an alcove with a staircase at the end of it. A sign on the wall said *To the Happy Shopper Rooftop Restaurant.* Owen dashed up the stairs. And found himself in the open air, surrounded by tables, about a third of them occupied. A waiter came over. Owen ignored him and scooted past. The waited yelled, "*Hey!*" and was about to give chase when Waverley appeared and shoved the man to one side. He span into a table and it collapsed under his weight, scattering broken crockery. People gasped, and one or two shouted.

Owen quickly realized he was trapped. There was no other way down except the stairs.

At least, no other way he liked to think about.

Waverley charged at him, sweeping furniture and shrieking customers out of his path. Owen backed to the wall at the edge of the roof. There were several potted plants on the ledge. Grabbing one, he threw it at Waverley, striking his shoulder. He wasn't surprised that it had no effect.

In the background, the public and staff were scrambling to escape down the stairs. A handful looked on, but none of them seemed likely to help. Owen was alone.

Then the furious alien was upon him. Owen punched and pummelled him, he kicked and scratched. None of it made any difference. The Waverley clone soaked it all up without so much as blinking. What remaining strength Owen had flowed out of him. He'd given it his best shot and he couldn't fight any more.

The alien bore down on him. It was over.

Poppy said, "Is that it?"

"Nearly," the secretary replied nervously. "I've never done this before."

"Well, get on with it. And I want the maximum volume." Poppy turned to the manager. "Give me the keys to the office."

The man fished a bunch out of his waistcoat and handed them over.

"Which one locks this door?"

He showed her.

The secretary said, "Er, finished. You just have to press this button."

"Right. Is that the only telephone in here?"

The manager nodded. Poppy ripped the wire out of the wall. He flinched.

She menaced them with her pocket-covered finger again. "I'm going to lock you in. If you so much as *touch* that Tannoy, I'll come back and shoot you. You won't turn it off, or down, or anything. Right?"

"Right," the manager whispered.

"Remember, I'll be on the other side of that door. Now hit the button, Doreen."

Outside, Poppy locked the door, pocketed the keys and hoped she hadn't frightened them *too* much.

She heard Owen's demo tape coming from speakers all over the mall. It started to have its effect as she headed for the escalators. Pseudo-humans succumbed to the tone as it cut a swathe of slaughter through them. And in dying, they revealed their true, horrible natures.

The real human beings, aghast, panicked. People ran in all directions, screaming and shouting. Poppy had to battle her way to the escalators through a stampeding mob.

She passed Leigh and Eric, twitching and foaming, and knew them to be counterfeits. Others, people she recognized and had worked with in some cases, twisted in pain and ... *reverted.*

But where was Owen? She searched as chaos reigned.

He was being choked and lifted off his feet at the same time. The Waverley clone seemed intent on throwing him off the roof.

"This is for what you've done to my kind," the alien rasped.

Then Owen became aware that life now had a soundtrack. And he was the composer.

The alien's face filled with horror and his grip loosened.

"And this is for what you've done to mine!" Owen said. His music boomed from the restaurant's speakers at full blast. The Waverley thing staggered back, clutching its throat, eyes bulging. It sagged to its knees. Owen reeled away from it. Then looked up, and saw a familiar face.

Poppy rushed to him and laid a hand on his arm. "You OK?"

"Yeah," he panted, "I think so." He nodded at the speakers. "Did you – ?"

"Yes. And it *kills* them, Owen. Look." She indicated the agonized alien. "Prepare yourself for a shock."

As it died, the creature cast off its synthetic appearance of humanity. It was everything human beings hated, everything they feared and had phobias about. It was insectoid, arachnid, reptilian, all rolled into one stinking carcass. It embodied all the horror of a creeping, crawling, unclean thing. It was a denizen of the worst dreams anyone had ever had.

But now the nightmare was over.

EPILOGUE

The afternoon sun glinted off the blades of the helicopter lazily circling above. Owen and his father watched as the military trucks set out, electronic music booming from the speakers mounted above their cabs. Ralph Saul came over with Leigh and Eric.

"How are you feeling?" Owen asked.

"I think we're all OK," the Professor replied.

"Yeah," Eric said. "It wasn't much different to being asleep really."

Leigh went to Owen and put her arm around his shoulder. They beamed at each other.

"Everything seems to be going very smoothly," Stewart Carter commented.

"That's one advantage of having government

contacts," Saul explained. "As soon as I got in touch with London they went on to emergency alert."

"Have we got all of them?" Leigh wanted to know.

Saul said, "If we haven't yet, we soon will." He turned to Owen. "I've been told there's to be a special session of the United Nations General Council later today. Item one on the agenda is to get your tape played on every radio, TV and satellite station in the world. That should flush them out."

A jeep pulled up and Poppy got out. "Hi, everybody!" she called. "How's it going?"

"Still mopping up," Owen said. "What about Waverley?"

"Believe it or not, he could be a changed man. He's very grateful for what you've done. And I think the experience just *might* get him to mend his ways."

Owen grinned. "The age of miracles is not passed. But he should be just as grateful to *you*. We all should."

Poppy shrugged and looked a little embarrassed.

Leigh had a question for Saul. "But won't their spacecraft things keep coming?"

"I expect they will at first. And we'll be ready for them. It shouldn't be too long before the message soaks in that this planet's not for taking. Until then, we keep watching the skies!"

Stewart Carter's mobile phone rang. "Yes? Oh, hello, dear. Yes, he's right here beside me. OK, I will." He handed the phone to his son. "It's your mother."

Owen took it and said, "Hi, Mum. What would you say if I told you my music's about to be broadcast to the biggest audience in history?"

His father smiled at him.